SPECIAL MESSAGE TO READERS

This book is published under the auspices of

THE ULVERSCROFT FOUNDATION

(registered charity No. 264873 UK)

Established in 1972 to provide funds for research, diagnosis and treatment of eye diseases. Examples of contributions made are: —

A Children's Assessment Unit at Moorfield's Hospital, London.

•

Twin operating theatres at the Western Ophthalmic Hospital, London.

•

A Chair of Ophthalmology at the Royal Australian College of Ophthalmologists.

•

The Ulverscroft Children's Eye Unit at the Great Ormond Street Hospital For Sick Children, London.

You can help further the work of the Foundation by making a donation or leaving a legacy. Every contribution, no matter how small, is received with gratitude. Please write for details to:

THE ULVERSCROFT FOUNDATION,
The Green, Bradgate Road, Anstey,
Leicester LE7 7FU, England.
Telephone: (0116) 236 4325

In Australia write to:

THE ULVERSCROFT FOUNDATION,
c/o The Royal Australian and New Zealand
College of Ophthalmologists,
94-98 Chalmers Street, Surry Hills,
N.S.W. 2010, Australia

THE WEEPING AND THE LAUGHTER

Kate Fielding — a widow, but still comparatively young — seems to have everything a woman could wish for in life — except someone with whom to share it. Then she meets and falls passionately in love with a young artist — Larry Stafford. Can their love survive the difference of a decade in their ages, the criticism of friends and of Kate's daughter, Roz, herself deeply involved with a married man? Can they overcome the terrifying illness which attacks Kate?

Books by Judy Chard
in the Linford Romance Library:

PERSON UNKNOWN
TO BE SO LOVED
ENCHANTMENT
APPOINTMENT WITH DANGER
BETRAYED
THE SURVIVORS
TO LIVE WITH FEAR
SWEET LOVE REMEMBERED
WINGS OF THE MORNING
A TIME TO LOVE
THE UNCERTAIN HEART
THE OTHER SIDE OF SORROW

JUDY CHARD

THE WEEPING AND THE LAUGHTER

Complete and Unabridged

LINFORD
Leicester

First published in Great Britain in 1975

First Linford Edition
published 2004

British Library CIP Data

Chard, Judy
The weeping and the laughter.—
Large print ed.—
Linford romance library
1. Love stories
2. Large type books
I. Title
823.9′14 [F]

ISBN 1–84395–209–2

Published by
F. A. Thorpe (Publishing)
Anstey, Leicestershire

Set by Words & Graphics Ltd.
Anstey, Leicestershire
Printed and bound in Great Britain by
T. J. International Ltd., Padstow, Cornwall

This book is printed on acid-free paper

1

As Kate walked up the steep main street of Kingsford, it started to drizzle. Her car was in the multistorey car park, and when she'd left home the weather had been warm, with a clear blue sky, a promise of intense heat to come, and she had on only a thin summer dress and no coat . . .

Later, when she thought back to that August day and all it had meant, she marvelled that such a small thing as that shower of rain should have changed the whole course of her life. So often it wasn't the big crises — death, birth, an accident — that altered everything, but something that at the time seemed so small, so insignificant as hardly to be noticeable.

As she climbed the hill now she noticed the board outside the Grammar School — 'Exhibition of local paintings.

Visitors welcome. Entrance 10p.'

On impulse she decided to go and see what they were like. She'd always wanted to see inside the building, part of it dated back to Queen Anne, her favourite period in architecture, also she was keenly interested in painting and pictures, although she had no gift for it herself. Also it would offer shelter till the rain stopped.

She hadn't exactly expected Royal Academy standards, but really most of these pictures looked like dabs of paint a child had done on whim. There were one or two flower studies, but even those looked more like designs for chintz — stylized, unnatural and stiff.

With a cursory glance at the rest she sank down on a wooden bench which stood in the middle of the make-shift gallery. Evidently it was really a wide corridor, almost like a cloister, which connected the old building with the newer one.

There was no one else about and she leaned her head back, the all too familiar weariness seeping through her limbs. She closed her eyes.

Suddenly she had the most peculiar feeling she was being watched. She opened her eyes. The place was still empty, and for a moment she couldn't understand the curious sensation she had experienced.

Then she saw him — he was staring straight at her from a plain light oak frame which hung opposite where she sat. She caught her breath — how could she have missed this one? It made every other painting in the place look like nothing . . .

Quickly she got to her feet, weariness forgotten. She looked closely at the portrait of the young man, she had to admit he was one of the most handsome young men she had ever seen, deep blue eyes and dark curling hair. The eyes were arresting, they seemed to hold a deep compassion, a shadowed sadness as if they had reached the depths of sorrow, encompassed and overcome it, and now the mouth was about to smile — life was really a joke — and she knew instinctively it would be a charming, warm, boyish smile.

But it wasn't just his looks. The arrangement of the features, the texture of the hair and skin, which the artist had reproduced with immense skill, and too he had brought out the depth of character, as in all good paintings — as she moved about the gallery to look at the picture from different angles — the eyes followed her . . . It was uncanny, as if the picture itself lived . . .

Underneath a card stated 'Portrait of the Artist'. That explained it, a self portrait. She wondered if the artist realized how much of himself he had disclosed . . . he couldn't be more than twenty at the most.

It was at that moment a voice broke into her thoughts.

'Well, do you like it? You've given it a flattering amount of attention!' The voice was deep and melodic.

She swung round.

And as if by magic waving of a wand, there stood the young man of the portrait, unmistakable, with those penetrating blue eyes. Now his hair was shorter and he was obviously older . . . but when he smiled there was no mistake, it was just as she had imagined it would be.

He was dressed in paint stained jeans and an open necked shirt, showing a deeply tanned chest. Kate felt herself blush, since Tom, her husband had died, five years ago, she hadn't been used to seeing any part of a man's body naked . . . for a moment the blood pounded through her pulses.

He held out his hand, 'I'm Larry Stafford — and I must add the picture was painted ten years ago — the card should really read 'Portrait of the Artist as a Young Man!' and I wouldn't say the original has worn all that well!'

Kate smiled. 'I'd still have recognized you, but I must be honest and tell you I only came in to shelter from the rain, although I'm interested in pictures and painting, and I'm thankful now that I did or I shouldn't have seen that portrait. It's really quite outstanding.'

He grinned, 'What about the rest? In a way I'm responsible for them too as I'm the Art Master here.'

Kate paused. She didn't want to hurt his feelings, for all she knew he was proud of the efforts of his pupils. As if he sensed her thoughts, he threw back his head and laughed — it was so infectious a sound that Kate had to laugh too, a thing she didn't seem to do often these days.

'It's all right, you don't have to flannel me, most of them are pretty awful, but at least some of them try, and I felt an exhibition would be an encouragement — you know, proud Mums can come and see their off-springs' efforts.'

Kate nodded, 'I remember when Roz was young — she's my daughter — we hoped at one time she might study art, but another interest in the shape of the horse, invaded her life — took over you might say — and from the moment she sat on her first pony, all else was lost!'

He smiled, 'I know, I suffer the same problems, the horse is my biggest rival! What is the fascination this animal has for the young of today I wonder.'

He glanced at his watch. 'Forgive me, I must grab some lunch before everyone else thinks about it.' He looked out of the tall windows, ' 'fraid it's still raining, but I can see a patch of blue the size of a sailor's trousers, if that's any consolation.'

Kate smiled at him, 'I haven't heard that expression since I was a child. Thanks for the optimism, I might as well wait now till it stops.'

With an airy wave of the hand he was gone. Kate returned to her hard seat, and contemplation of the picture.

For some reason she started to compare the young man with Tom . . . which was ridiculous for he would have been nearly fifty if he'd lived, she was forty herself, and this young man couldn't be more than thirty. But he had such an elusive charm, a lightness of spirit, with which something within herself found an answering chord.

Tom, much as she had loved him, had been inclined to be a rather serious person, for instance she couldn't imagine him laughing with quite such abandon as Larry had . . . already she thought of him by his christian name only . . . it suited him. She wondered if it were short for Laurence — or perhaps Lancelot . . . involuntarily she smiled — Sir Lancelot — no he wasn't at all that type.

Momentarily she'd forgotten the weather — now she noticed a shaft of sunlight through the rain spattered window, and she got up and went down the worn steps into the street . . .

She had nothing in particular to return home for, and as the clock on the town hall struck the hour, she decided she might as well have a light lunch at the cafe opposite the school.

She pushed open the door, to be greeted by a solid wall of heat and the smell of chips, but surprisingly, instead of repelling her, she found it gave an edge to her appetite as she stood looking round. The place was crowded, she couldn't even see one empty place. Then, suddenly, she saw an arm waving at her and there he was, sitting with a cup of coffee in front of him, the young man of the portrait . . . He was at a tiny table for two, squeezed into a corner by the coat stand, and she saw there was an empty chair opposite him. He'd got to his feet now, smiling, 'Come and join me, if you don't mind a bit of a squash. It's better than standing.'

She sat down and he held out the menu. 'I had plaice and chips, it was jolly good. Shall I go and get you some? It's a kind of self-service place — at least it's quicker that way.'

'Oh, I don't want to be a nuisance, and you're nearly finished . . . '

He waved aside her objection. 'Not to worry, the great outside world can wait an extra five minutes.'

When he'd gone she quickly got out

her powder compact and powdered her nose, added fresh lipstick, patted her hair into place. Suddenly it mattered how she looked . . .

The meal was surprisingly good.

'I suppose you're on holiday,' she said as she sipped the coffee he'd brought her.

He lighted a small cigar, then said quickly, 'I'm awfully sorry, do you mind? Living on one's own makes one forgetful of one's manners!'

She shook her head. So he wasn't married, that too suddenly seemed important. 'As a matter of fact I rather like the smell of those little cigars. Tom . . . ' she hesitated a moment, 'my husband always smoked a pipe . . . incidentally I know your name, but I forgot to tell you mine, it's Kate, Kate Fielding.'

He gave her a mock salute, 'I salute you Kate — or should I call you Mrs Fielding?'

'Please call me Kate.'

He put his head on one side,

considering her. 'Kate . . . yes, it suits you,' he said slowly, 'although I don't know, perhaps it's just a tiny bit severe, you're not a severe person are you Kate?' Suddenly the smile lighted up his face again, making Kate drop her eyes. Once more her heart quickened its beat, and she was filled with an extraordinary mixture of emotion which she couldn't analyse . . . but now she was near him, had talked to him, saw the painted image clothed in living flesh, his nearness seemed to fill her with an unaccountable longing for something . . . a flush of desire she'd forgotten was possible . . . and then a feeling of shame in case he should guess the thoughts that filled her mind . . .

But he was going on talking, answering her question, 'My job at the Grammar School isn't a very fat living, so during the holidays I take on any job that comes along — I don't mean only painting. In fact at the moment I'm helping with the harvest on one of the local farms. I like to get out in the fresh air as much as I can.'

Once more her thoughts flew to Tom. She'd always loved the outdoors, walking — even in the rain, but Tom, understandably tired perhaps at the end of a day at the office, just wanted to sit — in fact he was one of those people who could sit for long stretches of time doing absolutely nothing, while she herself needed activity, involvement, movement, action — Larry was like this she felt certain . . .

'Do you like music?' she asked suddenly.

'Yes, I love it, all kinds from Schmilsson to Schumann, the Beatles to Bach — not a very original statement, but true none the less. Do you?'

She nodded, 'Yes, I've the same kind of taste, although I must admit that I find some of the young pop stars a bit much to take!'

He laughed, 'Yes, but I guess crooners were condemned in their day, even Bing and Sinatra!'

For a moment Kate felt a little shiver go through her — Larry wasn't much older than Roz, her own daughter. Nearly a whole decade of living lay between them. She felt his eyes on her — 'More coffee?'

'No thanks. I must go and finish my shopping. It's been nice talking to you.' How banal that sounded for what she felt. 'If you've got any more pictures of your own — I'd love to see them some time — when you're not too busy . . . ' Directly she'd spoken she regretted it. It sounded so corny, as if she were chasing him, asking if she could go up and see his etchings, a bad music hall joke. But if he noticed her embarrassment he didn't show it. His face lit up with genuine pleasure.

'That 'ud be marvellous! If you wouldn't be bored. I do have quite a lot in the cottage where I live, not in any order I'm afraid, just canvasses stacked against the wall in the traditional manner!'

'Is the cottage in Kingsford or outside?'

'Down by the Quay.' He felt in his pocket and drew out a crumpled card and passed it to her. For a moment his fingers touched hers and an acute feeling ran up the nerves of her arm, almost as if she'd received an electric shock. She recognized the address, it was one of a line of cottages down by the estuary . . .

'Pop down tomorrow if you've nothing better to do, say about ten.'

She put the card in her bag and got to her feet. He opened the door for her, 'See you then.'

She stood for a moment, her eyes half closed against the brightness of the sun which was shining now from a cloudless sky, making dazzling golden pools on the steaming pavement.

She started to walk to the car park. She stopped for a moment outside the shoe shop, attracted by a pair of rather exotic looking sandals, proudly exhibited in solitary state on a stand. They were the kind a young girl would wear — but suddenly she knew she had to have them, Tom had always said she had beautiful legs.

Even as she tried them on she knew she was being foolish, they weren't particularly comfortable, and far from serviceable, as well as being a fantastic price for what was virtually a pair of soles and two leather straps, but in the mirror her legs looked slim and shapely, they could have been a young girl's legs — and suddenly it seemed to matter they should look attractive. She felt a suffocating sense of her own sex, a consciousness she never remembered having had before . . .

2

Next morning she drove to the quayside where a cluster of ancient cottages stood, once housing the men who worked in the local cider mill, long since pulled down to make way for a modern pub and Motel.

The tide was high and the water lapped and slapped against the stone sides of the quay. One or two boats tugged at their moorings, and herring gulls stood stiff legged, their yellow hooked beaks waiting to pounce on any odd piece of food or rubbish their bright eyes might spy.

She stopped the car a little way from the cottages, her heart was fluttering like a captive bird as she got out . . . His cottage was called The Moorings — rather unoriginal, but it had probably been called that since the first owner named it. It stood hunched between its neighbours as though they grudged it the space for one up and one down. The blue paint on the door and windows was peeling, the net curtains were dingy, and a pint bottle of milk stood on the step. A cat cleaned itself, sitting in the middle of a tub of scarlet geraniums. It was as if for a moment life stood still, as if the film in a movie camera had caught and crystallized for ever, that moment in time.

Larry opened the door to her knock, and she stepped into the tiny cluttered parlour. Although it wasn't exactly dirty, it was obvious no woman's touch lingered among the tubes of paint, the brushes, and bottles of linseed oil, the tea and coffee cups and cake crumbs. He moved a couple of canvasses off the seat of a chair, and dusted it with the sleeve of an old shirt.

'I've never seen inside these cottages before, I've often wondered what they were like, they're so charming from outside, and this is quite delightful, unspoilt . . . '

'It needs a lot doing to it, though. Money spent on it, painting and so on, and the worms and dry rot sent packing. But there are so many other things . . . ' He broke off, shrugging his shoulders. 'Never mind all that, what would you like to see — portraits, landscapes, or my 'blue' period?' He laughed down at her. How nice he could laugh at himself — that was something Tom . . . she checked herself quickly, feeling a stab of disloyalty to his memory . . .

Larry held up one painting after another, and there was no doubt they were good, she might even say brilliant from her small knowledge, which was mostly of classical paintings rather than the modern school. But there was something about these that appealed to her, caught her imagination, his inward eye interpreted exactly as did her own. They were imaginative, with a sweep of line, and intense richness of colour . . . some of the old buildings, the barns and roundhouses he'd chosen, were quite beautiful. What a pity they hadn't known him while Tom was still alive, they'd always meant to have a painting of their house done . . .

She turned to him, 'Larry, would you have time to do a painting for me? There's no hurry . . . '

'Is it of someTHING or someONE?'

'Of a house actually.'

'I'm willing to take on anything that helps me to eat and pay the rent,' he laughed, 'but I must admit I draw the line at still life — you know, a wine bottle, an apple and a piece of cheese! I see too much of that during term time. Portraits are really my thing, but houses, specially if they have character — I don't know I could work up much enthusiasm for a semi or a high rise block.'

'I don't live in either,' she smiled, 'and I think my house does have character. It's an old mill. But of course you'd have to see it before you came to any decision.'

Suddenly she was conscious he had

glanced at her legs, her skirt had wrinkled up when she sat down, she had on the new sandals she'd bought yesterday . . . she felt her cheeks burning, and quickly he looked away, tidying the canvasses. 'I could start next week, harvest'll be finished then and school is still a fortnight away . . . '

'It's only a couple of miles out of town, Brackenbury Mill. Maybe you know it,' she went on quickly, anxious to cover her embarrassment.

'I've only been in Kingsford just over 12 months, and apart from one or two farms I've worked on, I haven't got around the countryside much. But it sounds delightful.'

'Maybe, if you aren't busy that is . . . you'd like to come and see it now?' She held her breath. His reply seemed important . . .

'Fine. Just give me time to change my shirt, and I'll be right with you.'

He ran lightly up the steep stairs which were in a kind of cupboard in the corner of the room. Kate could hear him moving about overhead, whistling a pop tune. She thought — he's still so young — and I'll be forty-one next month. She tried to imagine what the bedroom was like, whether he brought girls here, whether indeed he had a girl friend.

He'd changed into a blue shirt that matched his eyes, and over it a velvet jacket as jet as his hair.

'I'd better follow you in Fred, only for the love of Pete don't do more than about 25!'

Seeing her puzzled face he said, 'Fred's my old banger, a great character, but not altogether reliable . . . '

When they got to the Mill, to the home she'd lived in all her married life, she suddenly felt shy and awkward with him, a feeling of inadequacy . . . but he was enchanted with the house. He wandered backwards and forwards, looking at it from all angles.

At last he stood on the lawn so that the old wheel could be seen to one side, and the water of the leat, with its cresses and rushes in the foreground, the house seeming to grow almost from within it.

'This view is perfect — that is if YOU like it,' he stood with his head on one side, a trait she was beginning to find endearing, as he weighed up the situation.

'Strangely enough it is one of my favourites, it used to be . . . ' she stopped. She was going to say, 'it used to be one of Tom's favourites too.' She wasn't quite certain why she hadn't gone on, said his name out loud, something had held her back.

They had coffee on the little paved terrace where Tom had set the old grinding stones from the mill as a centre piece, and honeysuckle and jasmine tumbled in sweet disorder over the walls.

Larry lay back in his chair, his eyes closed, the warmth of the sun on his tanned skin.

'Just listen!' he held up his hand, 'the most marvellous and priceless sound in today's mad, mad world — complete and utter silence. This is the kind of place one dreams about, but never finds. Hope I shan't be too tempted to lotus eat instead of working,' he squinted up at her where she sat, a little above him, on the wooden garden seat, the big coloured sun umbrella protecting her face from the glare of light — she hadn't wanted its harshness to show up the tiny lines round her eyes . . .

'I'll be a slave driver — big whip and all,' she laughed.

He was looking at her hands where they lay in her lap, at the wedding ring, the diamond and sapphire eternity ring Tom had given her on their tenth wedding anniversary. She was very conscious of his gaze . . . 'Is the painting to be a surprise for your husband?'

She looked away quickly, 'No. I'm a widow. Tom died five years ago.'

'I'm sorry. I had no idea. How clumsy of me.'

She turned and smiled at him, 'How could you possibly know? Anyway it's something millions of people have to learn to live with.' The calmly clasped hands belied the turmoil which he seemed to engender within her. He was still looking at her; quietly feeling for the right words, she said, 'I expect you know what I mean, the certainty that no one can ever take quite that place in your life again.'

He shook his head slowly, 'Not really. 'I haven't had a lot of love, of closeness — belonging, in my life.'

She wanted to ask him what he meant, but as if he were anxious to change the subject he said, 'Why do you stay on here, you must be lonely in such a big house, lovely as it is.'

She was silent for a moment, then she said, 'I suppose because in a way this is where all I want to remember, happened. That's company for me. And when Roz does come home, sometimes she wants to have friends to stay, and then four bedrooms aren't too many.'

As she talked about Roz, he watched her, listened as if he really was interested, as if he cared. She hadn't met anyone before to whom she felt she could talk like this. Even with Tom there had been times when she felt she couldn't communicate exactly what she felt.

'You see with an old house like this I often get the feeling that if I turn round suddenly, they'll all be there, the people who once lived here, and that includes Tom. I suppose in a way it's morbid to hang on to the dead, but I feel he is close in spirit to this place, which he loved so much.'

She paused for a moment, 'Even so, sometimes I do wonder what I'm to do with the rest of my life, in a way it seems to have no purpose, Roz really doesn't need me. People are wrong, I think, when they have their family as a kind of hostage to fate, it doesn't work that way, not always . . . '

He smiled lazily at her, 'Must there be a reason for everything? You can't return to, or recall the past, so why not settle for the present as it is? Just live one day as it follows another, enjoy it for what it is, sunny, cold, wet or dry.'

'Is that your philosophy for life?' she smiled.

He laughed again, and stretched his long limbs, 'I don't profess to have one really, but maybe it'll do till something better comes along. Meanwhile, how about having supper with me? We'll go down river to the pub, tide's right tonight, and I can always borrow a boat. It isn't the Ritz, but they do a good omelette, or a fresh crab salad.' He hesitated, 'that is of course unless you already have a date? I can imagine that someone like you has very few free evenings.'

She threw back her head and laughed, 'You have to be joking. I can't remember the last time I went out. Widows aren't popular as guests. They exist in a kind of No Man's Land, neither fish, flesh, fowl nor good red herring, and any unattached men in the party are always wary that they may be fair game!'

'In the summer I spend a lot of time gardening, in the winter I listen to records, read, go to the odd concert, hope Roz will drop in on me,' for a moment her eyes clouded.

His were full of compassion as he looked at her, 'It sounds rather sad, rather lonely, Kate. You shouldn't be a sad person, you should be happy.'

She glanced at him quickly, 'Do any of us deserve happiness unless we work at it? And then when it comes, do we recognize it?'

He shrugged his shoulders, 'I don't know, but I agree it is an elusive thing, fleeting as a butterfly. It comes unsought and when we least expect it. For instance sitting here with you, just talking, soaking up the sun, and drinking your delicious coffee — now that has been perfect happiness for me . . . '

For a moment she dared not meet his eyes. She got to her feet. The sun had gone behind a cloud, and she gave a little shiver. He jumped up and held out his hands, 'Let me take the tray for you, and then perhaps I could just wander round and get the feel of the house and garden, it may seem rather odd to you, but just as much character can appear in a painting of this kind, as in a portrait — if the painter can capture it!'

When he'd gone she went slowly up to her bedroom and opened the door of her clothes cupboard. For an hour she went through the dresses and suits — how dowdy and uninteresting they all were, colourless, an old woman's clothes — she needed some colour . . . she crossed the landing to Roz's room, she always left half her clothes there. She took out a white wool sweater, a pair of bright blue slacks and found a scarf to match, to tie back her chestnut hair . . . she changed and looked at herself in the mirror. The reflection showed shining eyes, a warm tinted skin — a woman who could have been years younger than she was. For a moment she felt a stab of doubt, it was a ribbed sweater and it clung closely to her breasts, as close as a second skin, but her figure was still firm, girlish . . .

He told her he'd call for her at six. She wandered from room to room, glancing at the clock, at her wrist watch, thinking the minutes would never pass, but at last she heard his car in the drive . . . she went out to the porch to meet him.

He opened the car door for her with a flourish, she could feel his eyes, full of admiration, resting on her . . . ' 'Fraid you have to loop that piece of string over the catch, Fred's seen his best days, but so long as he gets me from A to B, that's O.K.'

The engine seemed reluctant to start, and when eventually it coughed into life, it was so noisy that Kate soon gave up any attempt at conversation. He grinned at her, pointing to his ear and shaking his head as she tried to shout at him above the din. 'Not conducive to a cosy chat I'm afraid!'

The tide was high — a spring tide, so that the boats seemed almost to be bobbing about on a level with the wall of the quay.

'I'm afraid the boat I borrow from one of the fishermen is as much a veteran as old Fred, known with somewhat whimsical humour as the QE2! But at least I can row us home if the engine packs up, and what would life be without the added spice of uncertainty!'

It was ages since Kate had been down the estuary to Thurlecombe, the small fishing village which stood almost at the mouth of the river, sheltered from the south west winds by cliffs. She sat in the bow of the boat, watching the little curl of water, trailing her fingers in its cool greenness, seeing now and then a darting fish, while on either side the trees came down almost to the water's edge, and the fields rolled away, golden with fresh cut stubble, some of it already being burnt so that the smell of bonfires filled the breeze. And suddenly, just as Larry had described earlier, she felt a moment of complete and utter happiness, shining like a piece of quartz, every facet catching the sunlight.

The pub stood close to the water's edge, a stretch of fresh mown grass reaching down to the low wall where he tied up. He jumped ashore and put out his hand to help her. It was the second time he had touched her and she felt a little prickle of joy run up her spine . . .

It was early evening and the pub was still fairly empty. There were one or two people from the local Yacht Club. She and Tom had been members once, they'd had a small sailing dingy with an auxilliary motor, and when Roz was young, the whole family had enjoyed sailing, in fact Thurlecombe Regatta had always been the highlight of the summer holidays, the last excitement before school started.

A couple of them at the bar nodded to her, 'Good evening Kate. Haven't seen you for ages . . . ' Suddenly they realized it was a rather tactless observation as what they really meant was 'not since poor old Tom died . . . ' They glanced curiously at Larry, but she made no effort at introductions. Let them think what they like, she thought a little rebelliously, none of them had made much effort to contact her since she had been alone, and their eyes suggested her companion wasn't 'Quite their type' but for the moment she would forget the past, live in the present, absorb Larry's philosophy.

Suddenly she noticed one of the women whispering to a couple sitting with her at one of the tables, she laughed as she glanced at Kate — she was sure they were laughing at her — mutton dressed as lamb in the tight white sweater. She wished now she hadn't put it on. She pushed the hair back from her eyes where the wind had whipped the tendrils from the grip of the scarf. Probably thought she was baby snatching, she'd heard it in the past from their type . . . Then she thought with a flash of defiance — let them talk what do I care — there's no harm in just having an evening out . . .

As if he felt her discomfort, Larry suggested they take their drinks and sit on the low wall outside, watching the never ending coming and going on the water. Some of the boats rode at anchor, swinging round with the change of tide, some were coming in from a day's sailing, their crews brown and salt caked, some with galley lights burning as the enticing smell of cooking floated out of the portholes.

'Would you like to eat here, or go somewhere a bit more posh?' he grinned at her over the rim of his beer tankard.

'As I'm hungry enough to eat a horse, I think something here would be marvellous — whatever you suggest.'

She watched him as he swung away over the grass and back into the pub — lithe, supple, young. For a moment she let herself imagine what it would be like to be held in his arms, to feel his lips on hers . . . she pushed the idea from her and for a moment a little of the happiness faded, as if the sun had gone behind a cloud. This was something that could never be, something she should never have allowed to start. What madness was it had allowed her to pursue what could only be a dream, a transient rapture.

He came back with a tray loaded with fried scampi, brown bread and butter and a bottle of Rosé wine.

'Madame!' he bowed low, a white cloth over one arm, 'your dinner is served!'

They ate the tender pieces of shellfish with their fingers. Kate had never had a meal in a basket before — that showed how long it was since she'd been out — and for a moment she felt a sudden revulsion at the idea of eating without a knife and fork. Larry winked at her, 'Fingers were made before forks — it's the 'in' thing now, they even do it on the Costa d'Esmeralda, so I'm told!'

Tom would never have done this — once again a little flame of defiance flared in her — who cares? She thought, I'm enjoying myself.

He told her about his job at the Grammar School. 'I enjoy it up to a point, of course you get those who will never have any idea of what makes a painting live, no idea of colour or form, but if you get just one pupil who shows some kind of spark, who is keen, then that makes the whole thing worth while.'

'And you're fond of children?' she asked.

'All young people, yes . . . '

Kate smiled, 'I have to admit that looking round the gallery I found it difficult even to recognize what some of the pictures were meant to be!'

He laughed, 'I know, you like a nice orchard in spring with pink blossoms falling on skipping lambs, gambolling among the primroses!'

'As a matter of fact I do rather.'

He put his hand over hers, 'And why

not? Some people like Mahler and some the Beatles or Focus, some cherry tart and others caviar — every man to his taste, as the old woman said as she kissed her cow!'

Kate laughed so much the tears ran down her face. 'Where on earth did you get that terrible expression?'

'Oh from one of the farm lads I work with. 'Tis real Devon, m'dear!'

'Do you like working like that, casually, on farms?'

He shrugged, 'Not particularly, I can think of things I'd rather do, but at least I'm out of doors, and an Art Master at a school in a small place like Kingsford, that isn't Comprehensive yet, doesn't get a princely salary, and by the time I've paid my rent at the cottage, filled old Fred up with juice, there isn't much left for frills — not that I need many, but I do like the odd luxury like a ticket to a concert at the Festival Hall, or one of the new LPs, even though my record player would hardly come up to the audio experts' ideas of perfection.'

They sat on in the gathering twilight, his face a blur in the dusk, talking of this and that, exploring each other's minds, liking what they found.

'You know all about me and my family, now tell me about yours,' she said, trying to keep her tone light, to hide the deep interest and curiosity she felt.

'There isn't much to tell,' he paused to light one of the small slim cigars he smoked. 'I was put in an orphanage, what they call a Children's Home today, I suppose I was an illegitimate baby. No one ever told me,' he smiled at her, 'and of course in those days there was no permissive society, and adoption wasn't so closely controlled, or so popular as it is today. The nuns were kind, wonderful people. I'd been left in some kind of raffia Moses basket, I believe it was called, on their front door step. As all this took place in the county of Stafford, that was where my surname came from!'

She knew the compassion she felt for

the lonely child he must have been, showed in her eyes as she listened . . . and suddenly there was no laughter in his eyes, nor on his lips, as he took her hand. 'I'm going to see you again aren't I? I mean apart from the painting — as a . . . friend.' He turned her hand over, and bending his head, gently kissed the palm, so that for a moment she had an almost irresistible longing to cradle his head against her breast.

He got to his feet and held out his hand. 'Come on, we must go, or we shall find the tide has receded and left our boat hanging by its painter from the harbour wall — the ultimate disgrace for us seafaring folk!'

The little boat putt-putted gently back against the tide, and now Kate felt a shiver of cold, although the evening was still warm, the heat from the hills rising around them, as the silver drops of phosphorescence fell through her fingers like diamonds on the water.

Larry laid his arm along her shoulders as they sat in the stern of the boat, his old coat draped round her, so that she was surrounded by the aura of his very being, the smell of cigars, of soap, and linseed oil and paint, all mixed up with tar and salt — it seemed the very essence of this man, later she realized that perhaps that was the moment she fell in love . . .

The Mill seemed emptier, more silent even than it had before. Roz was away in Kent working at a training stables. At first when Tom had died she had rallied round her mother. She had only just left school and hadn't made up her mind exactly what she would do. It was to be something connected with horses — she'd never outgrown the Pony Club stage, Kate thought ruefully, simply progressed to something a little more mature and sophisticated.

How Kate remembered the terrible day they'd rung from Tom's office and told her, as gently as they could, the inescapable fact that he was dead. It had all been over in a few seconds, there was nothing anyone could have done, and at least, they said, she could console herself with the knowledge he had felt nothing.

Bitterly she had wondered what consolation that could be for the great yawning emptiness that her life seemed to become. Time hadn't seemed to take the feeling away — until now . . .

Jeff Baines, Tom's partner, had taken over the running of the Insurance Broker's office, and Tom had left everything in order as far as his private affairs were concerned, her future was assured to that extent . . .

Now she lay in bed in the empty house, the house Tom had brought her to as a bride, they had been so excited when they found it, an old mill house with the huge wheel still intact, although the leat that had driven it had long ago become overgrown and choked with weed.

Together they had lovingly restored the house, planted the garden, it had become part of the fabric of her existence and she couldn't understand how some women, fresh widowed, wanted at once to sell up their homes and get as far away as possible. Here were all her memories, here she could still imagine at times that Tom sat in his chair by the big open grate, his slippered feet stretched out to the blazing logs, even sometimes imagine she smelt his pipe tobacco on the evening air as she worked in the garden.

A huge August moon rose like a golden ball in the night sky, and flooded the room with light as she lay thinking of Larry, of the feelings that had so strangely filled her . . .

Soon after Tom had died had come the realization that youth didn't last forever, that she was approaching middle age, would soon even be old. They had seemed immortal to themselves, invulnerable in those years of early marriage . . . She still had very few grey hairs among the chestnut, her figure was slim and supple, she could play tennis, dance till the early hours perhaps . . . then after Tom's death had come the realization that people — places — everyday happenings that she had taken for granted were not indestructible — were indeed only part of a passing scene.

She would go grey, need to wear glasses, get the aches and pains of rheumatism, start to forget the details of day to day existence and repeat herself — all the things that she had thought only happened to other people . . . The poet had said, 'They are not long, the days of wine and roses . . .'

Tom had worked hard, in the early years they hadn't been all that well off and he was junior partner in the firm of Insurance Brokers, he'd had to prove himself, and like most of his generation, the war had taken some of his youth and energy.

Now she wondered if they had really been happy — she supposed so. Tom had slowed up in the last few months, got tetchy over little things, something he'd never done before, all of which, if she'd only thought, only known, could have been the signs of coming heart trouble.

She'd teased him once about being a bit of an old sobersides.

'All insurance bods are a bit serious, it's because we have to deal with so much death and disaster, the seamy side of life,' he'd said seriously.

She had always been the gayer of the two, not exactly frivolous, although there were times when she, like most people, would have liked to kick over the traces, done her 'thing' — although she wasn't too sure what it was. Travel perhaps, she'd never had much chance, when they were first married they couldn't afford it, then when Roz came along, it seemed too much of an upheaval, now she had the time and money, there was no one to go with . . .

Somehow the young today took it all in their strides, she envied them, they took it for granted it was easy to flit to the uttermost parts of the globe without so much as a backward glance, they were sensible enough not to get themselves cluttered with responsibility while they were young — maybe that was what made so many of them shy away from marriage . . .

Tom had been ten years older than she was, whatever they said, age did make a difference . . . but not so much if the man was the older . . . that brought her back to Larry . . .

The moon shone on her face. In olden days they said it turned you mad. Maybe she was a little mad, a kind of madness that affected women in their middle years — although she had no sign yet that the changes woman had to expect, were affecting her . . . for a moment the palms of her hands rested on the firmness of her breasts . . .

When at last she slept she dreamed that Tom was by her side again in the big double bed, that he held her in his arms, that their love rose to a crescendo of rapture — and then when she looked up into his face, it wasn't Tom at all, but Larry's and his young, strong arms that held her closely to him. And suddenly she wept for all the wasted years . . .

3

Now the days seemed to hold a new meaning for Kate. Each morning was filled with a kind of joyous anticipation instead of wondering how she would fill the long hours. She couldn't wait for the day to start, filled with the knowledge she would be seeing Larry. She had no idea where these feelings would lead, how it would all end, and she didn't care — she'd heard a song once — 'What's the use of wond'ring if the ending will be sad . . . ?' She was going to take the here and now, live every moment and enjoy it to the uttermost.

At her suggestion Larry came to breakfast each morning and started painting directly after. 'I bet you don't cook yourself anything,' she'd laughed at him as she put eggs, bacon, tomato and sausages in front of him, pouring herself a cup of coffee . . .

'Sometimes,' he said, his mouth full of sausage, 'just depends how much time I have and what's in the larder.'

She sat watching him, talking of this and that, delaying him from starting his painting, jealous in her heart of every moment he spent away from her. He worked all day till the light started to go, stopping briefly for sandwiches and a glass of beer or cider at mid-day, which she carried out into the garden. On days when the light was bad, or it rained, he'd work on the patio, under the glass roof, where Tom had planted the vine, filling in the odd shadows and parts of the mill wheel which he could do from memory.

Kate had cleared out a corner of what had once been a kind of garden room, which led on to the patio, and there he kept his paints, his easel, his brushes and an old paint smeared tweed jacket — all the paraphernalia of the artist. One evening when he'd gone home, she picked up a brush he'd dropped on the lawn, thinking with a little thrill of joy, that his hand had held it, and as she passed the old jacket where it hung on a hook, she laid her face for an instant against the rough tweed, and such an intense longing swept through her, she had to close her eyes against the dizziness.

He was adamant that while he painted he must be left alone. Kate tried to concentrate on some of the odds and ends she'd neglected in the house since Tom's death — making new covers and curtains, going to flower arranging classes, trying to behave normally, but all the time she was certain her feelings must show in her eyes, in her whole behaviour, in every part of her that was a woman, crying out, 'Can't you see, I'm in love, if only I knew that he loved me . . . '

Occasionally he would allow himself a busman's holiday, as he put it, and they would go to an exhibition of pictures, he'd discuss the different techniques, the styles, the masses of colour and form, telling her how he saw them from the artist's point of view, opening up a whole new world of interest, so that everything was different, as if she was seeing — really seeing — for the first time.

Then it was term time again, the painting of the mill was finished. Long ago she'd abandoned all pretence of it being a present — she was sure he must know the reason she had wanted him to paint the picture.

So once more the days started to drag a little. She'd ask him to supper as often as she could, and they'd listen to music, or just sit and talk in the gathering twilight. Sometimes at weekends they'd go out for a meal or spend all day Sunday in the country. Autumn was brilliant, a breathtaking September with blue, shimmering skies, it seemed it would go on for ever, almost as if summer were reluctant to leave the sun drenched fields and woods . . .

Kate would drive her little car up on to the moors — 'Honestly Larry, I don't feel Fred is reliable,' she'd laugh when he protested that he could drive, 'and we don't want to get stuck miles from anywhere,' she added. She'd pack a hamper of food and the old gas camping stove so they could cook in the fresh air.

One warm afternoon he'd taken the pins from her hair so that it fell about her shoulders, and taking her tanned face in gentle hands, kissed her on the lips. No words of love passed between them then, maybe both of them felt there was no need for words, Kate thought — but love wasn't a static thing, each hour of each day it had to move and expand, blossom like a flower, if it wasn't to decay and wither . . . was this just a passing fancy for Larry? A new experience, falling in love with a woman more than ten years older than himself? Dared she let herself care more deeply, get involved?

And still the long days lingered, each morning the sky was clear, the mist rose from the river, hanging low as the sun caught its surface and shimmered. Kate and old White, the gardener, swept up the gold and scarlet leaves and burnt them, filling the air with fragrance.

At the end of September Larry said, 'I'm going to paint your portrait, so you'd better find a good book to keep you sitting still, something long like *War and Peace*. Being a model can be very boring, and I want you relaxed . . . ' He laughed as he drove away in Fred, who was making more and more outrageous noises these days.

But Kate found nothing to bore her in the sittings, she was near him and that was all that mattered. Most of the work he did in the evenings when they'd had supper. Sometimes she'd load the record player with soft piano music, sometimes he'd talk as he worked, sometimes for two hours at a stretch he'd be silent, absorbed, until at last she had to move because her limbs were cramped. Then he'd be full of remorse. 'Kate, forgive me, I get so engrossed, I forget you're flesh and blood. Why didn't you shout at me?'

She'd make coffee while he cleaned his brushes. At first he wouldn't let her see the painting, but at last he considered it was far enough advanced for her opinion. She stood for a moment in front of the canvas, amazed at how he'd caught the expression in her eyes, she didn't realize her feelings spilled out of them to that extent. Was he telling her that he recognized the love in them? It was uncanny how clearly he had seen her thoughts . . .

'I don't know how much your fee for this is going to be?' She kept her tone light, not wanting him to see her expression until she had control of her feelings, 'hope I'll be able to afford it. Maybe I'll have to pay you in kind — feed you up!'

He came over to where she stood and took her hands in his, forcing her to look up at him, and once again she felt almost a shock as he touched her. 'As a matter of fact I think it's going to be the best thing I ever did,' he paused and smiled, dispelling for a moment the tension, 'so it'll cost a bomb.' He bent and kissed her gently, tenderly on the lips, and she closed her eyes against the wonder of it.

'Come and sit over here, Kate, and I'll tell you what the price will be.'

Such a tangle of emotions filled her, it was difficult even to hear what he was saying. Twilight filled the room, she hadn't wanted to light the lamps, destroy the intimacy of the atmosphere. His face was a pale blur in the dusk. Quietly, as if he were feeling for words, he said, 'Kate, you must have guessed I love you,' he hesitated. She tried to make some reply, but her mouth and throat were dry, the words wouldn't come. 'I know you feel perhaps that no one can take Tom's place, and time won't take that feeling away, but what it can do is to show you there is room for someone else in your life, someone who'll never want to usurp him because they'll want a place of their own in your heart.' Once again he paused. She saw him now through blurred eyes as tears pushed their way behind her lids. 'You can't think of being on your own the rest of your life,' he said so softly that she hardly caught the words, 'You were never meant to live alone, my darling Kate . . . .'

But now as he talked, whilst the joy at his words flooded through her, she could imagine she could hear the wagging tongues, the criticism, the dark forebodings of her friends — and Roz, what would be her reaction? She remembered the woman at the inn, smirking as she came in with Larry . . . there was not only the difference in their ages, but the fact that she was a comparatively rich woman, and that Larry had nothing but his rather poorly paid job at the school. All those thoughts thronged her head, but her heart cried out, 'Yes, Yes, I love you . . . I want to be with you always, to be your wife, more than I've ever wanted anything in my whole life . . . '

She got up and went across to the

french windows . . . but he hadn't said anything about marriage — not in so many words . . .

The big red ball of sun was setting in a glowing sky. Now she felt him move behind her, and suddenly she knew she didn't care, not about the wagging tongues, not if he didn't want to marry her — only to have his love, something that could be a thing of beauty for a little time even, then it would be worth it.

For a moment they seemed miles apart, then his hands touched her shoulders, turned her to face him. He didn't speak, but waited silently, watching her as the different expressions chased one another across her face like clouds on a summer afternoon. Until at last she smiled up at him and, putting two fingers on his lips, stood for a moment before he slipped his arms round her waist and drew her close. His cheek rested on hers, the dusk enfolded them, but the golden light of the setting sun still glowed in the shadows . . . At last she whispered, 'If it's really what you want, my love, then take the place in my heart where you belong . . . '

He kissed her gently and she could feel the beat of his heart against her breast as he said, 'Whatever may happen, whatever people may say, I love you Kate, with all my heart . . . '

And so it had begun, and she didn't care, or let herself think where it might end.

Then one evening a few days later she was at Larry's cottage, trying to tidy up. She'd made them some tea, while she waited for him to come from his afternoon classes — just like any ordinary wife, she thought with a little smile. She started to look through the stack of canvasses as she tidied them, they seemed to fill every available space in the cottage.

There was no doubt he had talent, maybe he was even brilliant, she hadn't enough knowledge to be sure, and of course she herself was biassed, to her they looked wonderful — she had a feeling, a kind of intuition about them.

She swung round when he opened the door, a canvas still in her hand. It showed a small chubby child, one of the local fishermen's children she guessed, tanned and naked with just a blue cotton hat on his golden curls as he bent, absorbed, to look at a jelly fish in a rock pool. You could almost smell the salt of the sea, feel the heat of the sun, touch the soft flesh . . .

'Larry, I've had a marvellous idea, let's have an exhibition of your work . . . '

He looked tired she thought, but he grinned, 'Where do you suggest we hold it — the Royal Academy, or just locally at the town hall, or the Grammar School? Don't think I'd be very popular with old 'Sunny' Somers, the head, so called in jest because of his exceedingly sour nature — and I doubt if I'd manage to get the Town Hall at this time of year, it's full of jolly leaping youngsters all doing their 'thing' to the latest pop records — Rave Ups I think they're called.'

She laughed, 'Just hold your horses, none of those places, let's use the old games room at the mill, it used to be a store, it's just the right shape — long with a low ceiling and a northern light. The walls are all whitewashed. It's full of old tennis racquets and croquet mallets, but I can soon clear it out . . .'

He bit into a thickly buttered scone, still warm from the oven, 'Croquet's a very 'in' game, why don't you set it up on the lawn and give parties in the shade of the immemorial elms!' he teased — she'd noticed sometimes he made little remarks to remind her of the difference in their positions in life . . .

She got up quickly, realizing he'd had a difficult time with his class. She went over and put her arms round him, nuzzling his neck. It was strange how she could do that kind of thing — show her love and warmth for him — she'd never been able to with Tom somehow, not to the same extent. Neither of them had been very demonstrative.

Maybe it was because she was shameless, maybe people were right about the rather pathetic sight of a sex-starved middle aged woman and a young man — she drew back quickly. But he caught hold of her and pulled her on to his knee — his tea forgotten . . . She laughed down at him now, suddenly secure in the warmth of his nearness.

'Don't evade the issue,' she said with mock severity.

'Darling Kate, I'm not, I think it's a marvellous idea, and Portrait of Kate shall take pride of place, just as the original does in my heart . . . '

Now his lips were on her mouth, gentle at first, then firm and more demanding and a longing, almost suffocating, the like of which she had never known, filled her so that every nerve in her body seemed to be tingling.

Sensing her response to his own desire, he gathered her into his arms as if she were a child, and carried her up the narrow, winding stairs.

Gently he laid her on the bed . . . for a moment she tried to protest, to reason with herself and him, though no words came . . . then the growing wonder of his love gradually swept all other thoughts from her mind, all other feelings from her body, so that the bud of her own desire, which had lain dormant so long within her, suddenly broke into blossom and all she could do was to utter his name in wonder and fulfilment.

Afterwards they lay in the golden warmth of the late sun, a delicious lethargy possessed her now, as she watched the motes dancing in the slanting rays, as he murmured tenderly, 'Kate, I want to keep you always, to have the right to hold you like this and never let you go — so maybe I will take you up on the idea of that exhibition. It might bring in some money — commissions even — then I would have a more reasonable income, so I could ask you to be my wife . . . '

His eyes, like two deep pools in the dusk, spoke of his love as she smiled up at him. 'Darling, don't be such an old square, you ought to know that these days it doesn't matter who has the money — Women's Lib. and all that . . . '

He kissed the lobe of her ear, 'Ah, but I am old-fashioned, and although I know you'll probably always have more money than I shall, at least I can do my part. At the moment it's all I can do to keep myself.'

She ran her fingers gently through the thick, dark hair, 'Whatever you say my love . . . '

The exhibition was an overwhelming success. They'd put an advertisement in the local paper. At first a small trickle of people came out during the week, when Kate would show them round, or just leave them to browse, on Sundays the drive was packed with cars that overflowed into the lane . . . Many people had wanted to buy Kate's portrait, but Larry was adamant, 'I'd almost as soon part with the original,' he laughed at her . . . but if he wouldn't sell that one, all the others went in the first fortnight — pictures of the fishermen working at their nets on the quay, sunsets across the estuary, a cornfield with an old-fashioned binder working round the headland — so lifelike you could almost feel the stiffness of the stubble, the buyer had said. He was a retired farmer, living in the town and missing the sights and sounds of the country. And now commissions started to flow in — particularly for portraits. Larry accepted as many as he could, but his school work had to come first . . .

And then one day he suddenly arrived at the mill at lunch time, bursting into the kitchen and picking Kate up, waltzing her round and round till she cried out, breathless with laughter and the hardness of his arms.

'Guess what! We're in the money. The Oil Moguls want me to do a series of pictures for the foyer in their new office building. They've offered to pay all expenses for me to go up to London for a couple of days to see the layout and discuss what they want. Rural scenes apparently, and seascapes, all subtly suggesting their products. Kate, this could be my big chance, the break through. And it's all thanks to you because you fixed that exhibition.' He paused for a moment and leant against the dresser, absently nibbling a carrot she'd been peeling.

'You mean they came down here and saw your work?' she asked.

'Apparently. It seems one of the senior Moguls came down to Cornwall shark fishing; one stormy day when the boats couldn't go out, they saw our advert, and he and his wife came over — the cunning types never said anything at the time, but apparently they bought the picture of the Jarvis kid, you know the little naked boy that you liked — the Board approved, and hey presto — approach is made to

Laurence Stafford . . . '

'I'm not surprised — Oh, Larry, how marvellous, when do you have to go?'

He held out the letter, 'Any time that suits me. I thought half term, I can get three or four days free then. Come with me Kate — we'll go to a concert at the Festival Hall, walk in the park, have dinner somewhere posh — just for a lark. How about it?'

He looked so young and happy Kate had to laugh.

'And no argument,' he pretended to look stern, 'it's to be my treat.'

For a moment she had caught his excitement and enthusiasm. She put her arms round his neck — 'Then I shan't come,' she teased, 'You'll have to go by yourself.'

His face fell, 'You don't really mean that?'

She shook her head, 'Don't worry, I'm not letting you loose in the wicked city without me. Let's make it a kind of celebration of . . . ' she hesitated and felt her face go pink, 'well, of our engagement . . . you arrange it all, I loathe booking rooms, getting tickets, and all that kind of thing, but please let me pay my share — for the hotel anyway . . .'

For a moment, as if he hadn't heard the last part of her sentence, he said, 'Rooms — did you mean that Kate?'

Although they were lovers she was still old-fashioned enough to feel a stab of something like shame at the idea of actually sleeping with him as man and wife in a hotel bedroom. It was something she and Tom had never done before marriage — making love in the privacy of Larry's cottage had been different somehow — but maybe this was part of the business — part of the price she had to pay as an older woman in love with a young man. The clash of principles must be inevitable.

She buried her face in his neck so he shouldn't see her eyes as she murmured low, so he only just caught the words, 'Then I'll change the word to room in the singular, if that is what you want, my darling.'

Once or twice in the week before they were due to go to London, she had a little niggling doubt, tempted almost to say she wouldn't go after all, then, like a young girl in the flurry of her first affair, she remembered how it had been that evening in the cottage, remembered the feeling of his lips — and knew she would go.

To begin with they were a little stiff and formal with each other — she'd never seen him in a suit before, always a sweater and jeans, or at best, a pair of slacks — now he was resplendent in a dark grey suit with a pale blue shirt and a spotted bow tie . . . She'd put on a dress with a matching coat and a wide brimmed hat — she hadn't worn the outfit for years, in fact so fickle is fashion, it had swung back again and even the length of the skirt was right. Suddenly they caught sight of each other reflected in a shop window and started to laugh. 'I hope all this money and fame isn't going to make you too posh,' he said, squeezing her arm.

She laughed back at him, 'Well of course when we go to get your decoration from the Queen for services to the Arts — we'll have to look our best . . . '

It was in this lighthearted mood they reached the hotel. It was small and cosy, a place Larry had chosen. Their room looked out over an old-fashioned London square — seldom found these days, with green painted wooden seats, and trees, and people exercising their dogs. It was kept neat with clipped shrubs and no litter lying around on the paths and grass, the plane trees shed scarlet autumn leaves, and the pigeons cooed soothingly on the roof tops.

Larry had booked tickets for a piano recital and concert at the Festival Hall for their first evening, and Kate felt a little surge of excited anticipation as they sat waiting — the musicians taking their places while programmes rustled and people coughed and chatted as they settled into their places. Then the slow chords of the concerto opened, leading into a romantic melody and she closed her eyes and let the music sweep round her, such music as she had never really heard before from a full orchestra in concert, for Tom had never really enjoyed classical music, and now with the magic of Larry's presence near her, she was filled with the richness and emotionally stirred so that it engulfed her . . .

When at last it ceased and the concert was over, she hardly realized where she was as a great wave of applause crashed like thunder through the hall, and she felt almost tipsy with the splendour. It helped to dispel any qualms she might have had as later Larry took her in his arms, and there was nothing but their love and his voice as he whispered her name like a caress.

4

It was strange the next morning to wake to the hum of traffic after the quiet of the country, which she had known so many years. There was the constant buzz of the huge planes overhead, on their way to and fro from London Airport, and she thought about the people inside them, and wondered where they were going, and if they were as happy as she was. Larry was still asleep. He lay with one arm flung along the pillow by her shoulders, his long dark lashes curling on his cheeks, and for a moment she felt an overwhelming rush of love and almost maternal protection, he looked so young, so vulnerable . . .

They ate a leisurely breakfast, and all the time she was conscious of the look in his eyes, of the love that flowed between them, of the supreme happiness he had brought her . . . then suddenly she turned her head and became aware that the woman at the next table was watching her. She must have been about her own age, opposite her was a balding plump man, who Kate supposed was her husband. For a moment she saw envy in the woman's eyes as she watched her with Larry, then she gave a slight grin as contempt drew down the corners of her mouth. She turned to her husband, hidden behind the morning paper, and whispered something. He lowered the paper and glanced across at Kate and Larry, murmured something, which made the woman giggle, and then went back to his paper.

For a moment Kate felt a surge of anger, she would like to have knocked the silly smirk from the woman's face, to have said, 'Yes, he is younger than me, but I don't think it matters, I love him and he loves me . . . ' She would like to have forced the words she was sure had been spoken, back down her throat . . . but at last contempt replaced fury, that anyone could be so petty. But the pleasure had gone out of the day . . . would she always be so vulnerable, always be thinking, perhaps imagining, that other people were talking about her? Criticising the difference in their ages — and was it so obvious that a total stranger should notice?

Larry was off to see his Oil Moguls. In his excitement he didn't notice her preoccupation. He kissed her lightly, telling her not to buy up the whole West End on her shopping spree.

When he'd gone she went slowly upstairs to get her coat. She had thought of walking along the King's Road, having a look in some of the boutiques, going to Biba's perhaps, but the woman had suddenly made her conscious once again of her age — the matronly departments of the big stores in Oxford Street would be more appropriate — she was a middle aged woman, with a grown up daughter

— nearly the same age as her lover. A feeling of self-loathing suddenly swept through her so that by the time she reached her room, the tears were running down her cheeks. She bathed her face in cool water, re-did her make-up, it was too ridiculous to let some strange woman in a hotel dining-room get under her skin . . .

She looked critically at herself in the mirror. The sun was bright outside, the early November morning still crisp with the night frost that lingered in the shadows. Her skin was clear, her eyes bright — but there were tiny lines around her eyes — the hint of a wrinkle across the smoothness of her forehead. Quickly she put on her make-up, brushed mascara on her lashes, put on more eye shadow than usual with a gesture of defiance, and going into the busy street she made for the Underground — and Kensington.

When they got home there was a letter from Roz. She wrote that she was coming home for a few days before taking the horses to America from the stables where she worked. These days show jumping seemed to have no season, she added, and when they finished in England, then it meant jetting to Europe, to Russia, to Japan — and now she was one of the head 'lads' in the stables with quite a slice of social life to lead and she needed some clothes . . .

Kate felt a stab of guilt. In her new found happiness she'd thought so little about Roz. She was a part of her life that seemed not to belong to the past, almost like a chapter that had closed. She had mentioned Larry to her in her letters, but nothing of their relationship, just as an artist she'd had to paint a picture of the mill — no more no less. And yet of course to say she was part of her past was wholly ridiculous. Roz was her child, her own flesh and blood, all she had left of Tom . . . it was just that somehow they seemed to have grown so far apart, they were almost like friends instead of mother and daughter.

Meanwhile some kind of bush telegraph system had worked in the village and surrounding countryside, even as far as some of her acquaintances in Kingsford, and it wasn't long before they were dropping in, ostensibly for a general chat, but always coming round to the subject of Larry. The ones who had known her in the days when she was married to Tom were full of dark forebodings, particularly Mary Hallett, widowed like Kate, who had said, 'Look, I've known you long enough to speak my mind, are you sure he isn't just after your money? The security you can give him? These artistic types are often a bit feckless you know.'

With difficulty Kate had kept her temper. The trouble was in her heart of hearts she was often assailed by the very doubts that Mary had expressed in words, but she said, 'No Mary, of course I'm not sure, you may well be right, no more than I was sure Tom wouldn't go off and leave me after a few months — it's a risk we all have to take in human relationships — but I don't really care, I love Larry, and I'm in love with him, there's a vast difference, but for him I feel both emotions perhaps more deeply than I ever felt for Tom even. I'm content with that.'

Mary got up and came over and kissed her, sighing as she did so. 'Well, I hope he feels the same, love. I know it's none of my business, but I am very fond of you, still it's your life . . . '

Kate was strangely touched by her words. 'Thanks Mary, I know what you must think of me but maybe one day it'll happen to you then you'll understand how I feel, that it's a kind of gift from heaven that I'm grateful for, whatever the outcome.'

Since Tom had died Kate had dropped out of most of the social life of Kingsford and the village, such as it was. Tom had belonged to the golf club, they'd had the odd bridge evening, but most of the people had been partly business acquaintances, they hadn't had any really close friends, apart from Mary and her husband, and of course Jeff Baines, Tom's partner, and his wife, Meg, and the latter stuck by her now, whatever may have been their private opinions.

She asked them over one Sunday morning for drinks to meet Larry. At first the atmosphere had been a little strained, after all it was a rather awkward situation — Jeff knew all about Kate's financial affairs, more than Larry did, and he knew too she was a comparatively rich woman — but he was determined to keep an open mind. He told Meg after, 'I like Larry, there's something about him that's four square, honest. And Kate's said nothing about wanting to make her money over to him or anything like that. She's still a pretty level headed woman, even if she has fallen for a younger man!'

'I wouldn't mind him myself, bach,' Meg teased, her Welsh accent pronounced as she laughed up at Jeff, knowing that he knew she would never even cast a glance at another man. 'Real dishy, and anyone can see with half an eye they're lovers — she looks like a cat that's had a whole bowl of cream, never mind a saucer. I'm only jealous really, romantic old me, and I wish her all the happiness in the world. It couldn't happen to a nicer person.'

Kate had told Larry of Mary's remarks. He drew her into the circle of his arms.

'Look my love, you're bound to get this kind of thing, with all due respect to your fair sex, women are like that — and men sometimes too,' he added as an afterthought, 'but we're both free, beholden to no one, we are entitled to do exactly as we like, nothing can spoil what is between us.' His lips were on hers, warm and demanding, and she responded, feeling the mounting passion, but gently she disengaged herself, she still couldn't bring herself to let Larry make love to her where she and Tom had loved and lived, where Roz had been conceived and born — something — some fastidiousness perhaps — held her back, just as she could only imagine Larry beside her in the big double bed in her dreams — not in actuality.

And now there was a light step on the paved terrace and a tall fair girl stepped through the french windows, her hand on the frame for a moment she paused, looking at them, a slightly startled expression on her face . . . Kate held out her arms, 'Roz darling, how lovely — but I wasn't expecting you till next week.'

After a moment's hesitation, the girl went over to her mother and kissed her lightly on the cheek, 'I know, but we had to alter the arrangements, so here I am.' She turned and looked at Larry with open curiosity. 'Aren't you going to introduce me?'

'Of course,' Kate sounded a little breathless. It must be obvious to Roz that the atmosphere was highly charged, and indeed Kate didn't know how long she'd been standing there, how much she'd heard of their conversation — not that it mattered, she would have to know the position, but Kate had wanted time, to do it her own way, not be hurried . . .

'This is Larry, Larry Stafford. I did tell you in my letters — he's been doing a painting of the house, in fact there it is.' She pointed to where the canvas stood on the mantelpiece, as yet unframed, glad for a moment's respite as Roz went over to look at it. Kate turned to Larry, 'As you must have guessed, this is my daughter Roz.' Her smile was a little tremulous.

He nodded, 'It doesn't take much imagination to see that,' he said softly, 'she certainly has her mother's looks, specially about the eyes and mouth.'

Kate went over to the drinks cabinet, still feeling a little shaken by Roz's sudden appearance — supposing she and Larry . . . 'I hope you're going to stay for a little while,' she said quietly.

Roz turned and smiled, 'I'll be here

for two or three days — Dick — Mr Fordyce, is taking four horses to Massachusetts to the show there — and I'm going along too, that's why I need some new clothes . . . ' she hesitated as though she was going to add something, then took the glass of sherry that Kate held out, and dropped her eyes.

Kate perched on the arm of a chair, a little uneasy. She so hoped these two were going to be friends, and yet she knew Roz could be difficult . . .

Roz stretched lazily like a cat, 'I'd love a bath Mum, and a change of clothes, I seem to live in jods and breeches, and the bathing arrangements in my flat over the stables are a bit archaic.' She laughed at Larry, and for a moment he had a glimpse of what Kate must have looked like at her age. 'I like the painting very much, reminds me a bit of Van Gogh's orchard — but in fact I think I like yours better!'

Larry grinned and saluted her, 'Thanks for the compliment. I'm a great admirer of Vincent myself, and

I'm always teasing your mother she likes pink blossoms and skipping lambs.' They all laughed and there was an easing of the tension.

'And I suppose that's a self-portrait?' The girl pointed to Larry's original painting of himself.

He nodded, 'As you can see, I was a whole lot younger then. It doesn't look as if I liked the world as it was much either does it? Still, ten years had knocked some of the edges off I think. I must say though I envy the young today, like you, the world is your oyster, and the travelling you can do is guaranteed to soften the edges even more.'

For a moment Roz's eyes met his challengingly, not sure if there was more behind his words than seemed apparent. Kate broke the spell by saying she must go into the kitchen and rustle up some food. Roz got up and followed her. When they were safely behind the closed door, she said, 'He's nice, Mum, your fella. Going to marry him?'

Kate felt herself blush at the directness of the question. No beating about the bush with the young nowadays. 'I think so, yes.'

Roz grinned and then turned her head quickly, playing with the stem of the sherry glass she'd brought with her, then draining it she said, 'Good-oh. It's a nice old-fashioned custom.' Kate thought she could hear tears, and a trace of bitterness in her voice, but before she could say anything, the girl had turned and run up the shallow oak stairs, whistling a pop tune, slightly off key.

Kate stood in the kitchen, a feeling of helplessness sweeping over her, Roz had often made her feel like this. Since a child she had been inclined to be at odds with things and people . . . maybe being an only one she and Tom had spoilt her, in fact that was why they had sent her away to boarding school, but maybe that had been a mistake. She could remember the first summer holidays, Roz had seemed withdrawn and serious, as if suddenly childhood had gone. Kate had heard her weeping one night, and managed to get it out of her that she thought she'd been sent away to school because Kate was going to have another baby, a baby who would take her place — she'd felt rejected, unwanted. As it happened Kate had been pregnant, but she'd had a miscarriage — but all that had had nothing to do with Roz being sent away to school, that aspect had never even entered hers and Tom's heads, as she tried to explain. But their relationship had undergone a subtle change from then on, it was as if Roz felt she couldn't trust her mother. Kate tried to find out if something had been said at school, adolescent girls could be very cruel — and then at the end of the holidays a small and silly incident had occurred which had remained in Kate's mind.

They'd gone blackberrying at their favourite spot up on the hills near

Branscombe Farm, and on this particular afternoon some other people had got there first, which they were quite entitled to do, but Roz had been beside herself with fury. She shouted at them, 'Serve you right if you die of poison. All these bushes have been sprayed with weedkiller.'

Kate had turned to her, 'How do you know that Roz?' The girl had looked sheepish for a moment, then she said defiantly — 'I don't, but they're ours — I don't want anyone else to have them.'

Kate had made her go and apologize and the people had laughed it off, but Kate had never forgotten the pain and anger — more like a grown up's face than a child's.

Now sometimes she was like the old Roz, then suddenly she'd withdraw, be almost sullen, shrugging her shoulders when Kate asked if she'd like her to come with her to buy the clothes she needed. 'Please yourself,' she'd say.

Then occasionally she'd open up,

'Dick's let me do quite a bit of actual show jumping lately, mostly with novices, I'm not up to competition stuff yet. It's eventing I'd really like to do . . . ' her eyes shone for a moment, 'help him make a name . . . '

Kate folded clothes in tissue paper — 'Honestly Roz,' she laughed, 'this is more like a trousseau . . . ' the words were hardly out of her mouth before she heard a sound behind her, half sob, half choke . . . she swung round and was horrified to see tears streaming down Roz's face. She went over quickly and put her arms round her, feeling the body stiffen for a moment before she relaxed a little. 'Darling, what on earth's the matter? What did I say? I didn't mean . . . '

Roz's face crumpled like a small child's making her look so endearingly vulnerable that Kate was near to tears herself.

For a moment Roz sat with her mother's arms about her, then she said, 'I'm sorry Mum, I didn't mean to be feeble, it's just that I'm so in love — in love with Dick. I've never felt like this about anyone before, I didn't know it was possible. I just can't help myself . . .'

Kate didn't speak for a minute, she knew the feeling only too well. But of course Dick Fordyce was married . . .

'I didn't mean to spoil everything by telling you,' Roz hesitated as though she was going to add something, then she blew her nose and stood up. 'Well, now you know, still not to worry, I guess I can look after myself,' she said with forced brightness, 'and it isn't a very original theme — young girl falls for older married man, you read about it all the time — I expect things will sort themselves out . . . ' She paused for a moment, then said with a note of defiance, 'You marry your Larry, Mum, and be happy. I reckon it's only seeing you two lovebirds together made me feel jealous,' she gave a watery smile, 'not a very nice feeling.'

Kate felt desperately inadequate. She

felt too that Roz was holding something back . . . but she knew it would be useless to probe . . .

In the days that followed they didn't talk much, the hours seemed to fly by, filled with packing, getting visas, injections and so on, and at times it seemed Roz had built a little shell round herself which warded off questions . . . it wasn't easy to communicate with her again. It was almost as if Roz were terrified of letting her mother see any hint of softness in her nature. Once or twice Kate thought she heard her crying in the night, she longed to go and comfort her, but was afraid of destroying the fragility of their relationship.

Then on her last day, with a flash of the old Roz, she said, 'I suppose marriage does work for some people, you and Dad had some good years . . . '

'Of course it works,' Kate said more sharply than she meant, she too was vulnerable, 'it's just that one only hears about the failures, the others aren't of much popular interest.'

'Maybe men have changed since you were young,' Roz said with a trace of the old bitterness, 'or I attract the wrong ones, the ones whose feelings are shallow, purely physical perhaps, but Larry isn't like that is he?'

Kate avoided her gaze for a moment, then she said slowly, 'No, I don't think so, maybe . . . ' she was going to say, maybe it's the kind of people you mix with, or maybe it's my fault, mine and Tom's that we led you to expect too much . . . but Roz had to live her own life, it was something parents couldn't do for their children, all they could hope was that they would find true happiness somehow.

She drove off with the little scarlet Mini piled high with boxes and cases, promising to be back in a month, in time for the wedding . . .

Kate watched her go, a sudden fear in her heart for no reason. Maybe it was as well she didn't see Roz draw into the first layby she came to and, stopping the car, drop her head on her hands, crying out in an agony of despair, 'Oh, Dick, Dick, what am I going to do!'

5

It seemed as if the whole tempo of Kate's life had changed, quickened . . . Larry received so many commissions as a result of the exhibition that he had told the headmaster of the Grammar School he would be leaving at the end of the winter term. But first he had to complete the half dozen pictures the oil company wanted, and for which they had paid him a large sum of money in advance — thus making his resignation possible.

He worked every spare minute he could, Kate was glad she'd persuaded him to use the studio at the Mill, otherwise she could seldom have seen him. As it was, he was usually so tired when he finished, he could only swallow some food she prepared, and drive home to flop on the bed and be immediately asleep. He knew his work at school must be suffering, but it was just one of those things, Kate had pointed out that his personal career must come first, and these particular paintings were too good an opportunity to miss.

She felt sure the pictures were quite brilliant — there were landscapes and seascapes mostly, all in some way showing the use of oil in its many forms in daily life . . . 'They're my kind of pictures,' she laughed at him, 'Kentish oast houses, cherry orchards, Cotswold fields and woods.'

He stopped for a moment to kiss the end of her nose. 'At the end of term I'm going to take a break, so prepare yourself, we'll get married before Christmas and still have just a week for a short honeymoon . . . '

She drew back for a moment. Now it was imminent it seemed so final, such a big step — marriage. As far as she was concerned she knew the meaning of the vows she would give to Larry, but he was so young, did he realize what he was taking on? In sickness and in health . . . till death us do part . . . ' It was odd that particular phrase should come to mind, she'd always been the healthiest of people, but ten years was a big gap . . .

Larry had gone back to his painting and was putting the fine edge on a storm cloud — he didn't notice her momentary withdrawal. 'Roz'll be back by then won't she? I read somewhere the horse junketing or whatever in America, ended last week.'

Kate nodded. She'd had one air letter from Roz since she left. It was brief and impersonal . . . it seemed the show had gone quite well and they'd be staying on a few days after, they'd met some people Dick had got friendly with and wanted to see their American bred fillies 'out in the Blue Grass Country'. Kentucky to you and me! Roz added. 'We drove to Washington . . . it's strange how quickly one gets used to the American countryside, at first it seems all marvellous and surprising, then you become somehow sated, almost blasé — you just can't be amazed any more. In fact I feel almost as if I've been in America most of my life! And the people here think nothing of driving long distances, just 'to visit with someone'. But mostly they fly, it's just they like to show us 'foreign cousins' the countryside. You know how in England we still find long distances quite an undertaking, but over here where the big cities are farther apart, to them it's just an afternoon's outing!'

Kate read the letter over and over again, trying to glean some hint of how things were going with Roz and Dick personally — but it could have been a letter from a mere acquaintance. The only thing it really did was to make her long to see the places and scenes Roz described . . . Maybe one day she and Larry would be able to travel, to see parts of the world she'd only read about. That was one of the advantages of making a living as an artist, it didn't really matter where you worked from . . .

It would of course be a very quiet wedding — Kate would really have liked to slip away to an impersonal register office in London, but she knew it would deeply hurt people like Mary, and Jeff and Meg not to be present, also it meant complications over licences and so on. They had discussed whether it should be in church, or the local register office. Kate felt if they had it at the church, where she and Tom had been married, where Roz had been christened, it would be awkward, she couldn't face the curious glances of the people she had known, at least in a Register Office it could be a private affair, with only those present they wanted to ask.

The clothes she had eventually bought while she was in London were a compromise between the boutiques and the big stores — she'd allowed herself the luxury of a rather trendy hostess gown in clinging silk jersey with a very low halter neckline — she didn't know if she'd ever dare wear it, she'd also bought a black lace nightgown and a wrap to go with it, edged with white fur . . . when she got home she'd tried it on, but she'd hardly glanced at herself in the mirror before she wrenched it off, bundled it up and pushed it into the back of her cupboard, convinced she'd never wear it. The ordinary nighties she'd worn all her married life were much more sensible for a woman in her forties, she told herself sternly.

She'd also bought a blue dress with a matching long suede coat and a little suede hat, the price had nearly made her faint, but she felt they were just right to be married in and to go away after. She'd ask Roz if she approved. It was a weight off her mind that at least her daughter and her future husband approved of one another, and Roz didn't seem to resent the fact she was going to marry again, although she had idolized Tom. They had always been very close, much closer than she had ever been with her own daughter, often there was an affinity between father and daughter . . . maybe in part she would be able to renew it with Larry. If only she hadn't got herself involved with this Dick Fordyce. Still perhaps by now the glamour might have tarnished a little . . . she could only hope so.

Roz arrived a few days before the wedding. Larry had finished his teaching, and completed the first part of his commission for the Oil Moguls as he called them.

Kate studied her anxiously, she looked taut and drawn like a violin string, she was edgy and on the go all the time as if she couldn't sit still, smoking one cigarette after another. It was obvious she was making an effort to fit in with the happiness surrounding Kate and Larry, but there was a brittle kind of quality about her laughter, and her smile didn't quite reach her eyes . . . Kate longed to talk to her, but she seemed more withdrawn than ever. At least she took an interest in Kate's clothes — although she didn't show even her the dark secret which lay crumpled at the bottom of the cupboard in her bedroom.

Kate was surprised when she saw the inside of the Register Office. She'd expected a drab and ordinary place like a solicitor's office, but there were pale cream walls, a deep chocolate carpet, and bowls of flowers. Jeff and Meg, Mary and Roz were there and just before they left the Mill Roz had kissed Kate and produced a small bouquet of violets and anemones which complemented the blue of her dress . . . Kate felt the tears prick behind her eyelids . . . laughingly Roz gave her a tissue, 'Hey, that won't do, your mascara will run!'

She seemed in a kind of dream as the formalities were gone through, it was all hazy and somehow unreal, so unlike the marriage service in church . . . but now it was an accomplished fact, and there was no turning back. Larry kissed her, his lips warm on the coldness of her face, and she could smell the new after-shave she'd given him . . . 'Oh, please God, let me make him happy,' she prayed, closing her eyes for a moment against the December sun-light . . .

They drank champagne, and ate roast duck, followed by strawberries and cream, the waiter telling them the fruit had been flown from France.

'How wickedly extravagant!' Kate exclaimed, smiling at Larry over the rim of her glass, she wasn't really used to wine and she felt quite tipsy — but happy and carefree, almost like a girl again. If only Roz didn't look so stricken. She made an effort to join in the laughter, the gentle teasing, but now and then Kate saw an expression of almost physical pain cross her face when she saw Larry with his arm round her mother, squeezing her hand, looking down into her eyes, his own full of love . . . Kate longed to soothe away the troubled look as she had done when she was a little girl, and try 'to make it all better'. But she knew this was something that only Roz could resolve for herself.

She had told Kate she would stay on at the Mill till they returned from their honeymoon. Larry felt he could only spare a week from his easel until the present commission was finished, 'We'll have another proper honeymoon come the summer,' he said, pulling her to him and kissing her deeply and longingly . . .

And so she tried to think that Roz would work her life out all right, jealous now of her own precious happiness.

They said good-bye and Larry took the wheel of Kate's little car, piled high with suitcases. 'You'd think we were going on a world tour,' he'd teased her as he loaded up the cases, 'instead of a week in the Cotswolds.'

She'd blushed for a moment as she thought of what they held, 'well you never know in this country what the weather's going to do, today it's just like spring, tomorrow may bring a blizzard.'

He tucked his sketch block and coloured pencils into the pocket of the car, and she felt a lift of the heart in joyful anticipation of the hours alone with him that lay ahead . . . it was fortunate she couldn't see Roz's stricken face as she threw herself on her bed as soon as they had left, or hear the agony of the retching she endured each morning. She had made a superhuman effort to appear normal, now she could let the agony of remorse take over.

They had booked into a private country hotel, hoping for privacy at this off season time of year, and both of them loved the Cotswolds . . . it was a converted country house standing by itself in a wooded parkland, part of which had been ploughed up, obviously for crops, but either side of the driveway was a formal kind of garden with a croquet lawn in front of the gravel sweep by the house. Larry threw back his head and laughed, 'There Kate my love, we shall be able to have a dignified and leisurely game of croquet after breakfast, providing the weather holds . . . how does that grab you, Mrs Stafford?' He smiled down at her with shining eyes.

She had pulled off her hat and tendrils of hair had escaped the pins, framing her face, which he now took tenderly between his hands. It was the first time anyone had called her by her new name and it sent a little thrill of pleasure and excitement along her nerves. He drew her into his arms and kissed her hungrily on the mouth. 'Kate, my darling Kate, my wife — I love you so much, so very much . . . ' She returned his kiss, and then felt a little stab of embarrassment in case anyone should be watching from the windows.

'They'll see us — guess we're just married . . . '

He lifted his head, 'Who cares? Let's tell the world.' He jumped out as if he were about to do just that, then ran lightly up the steps to the front door, but before he could knock it was opened by a middle aged woman in sweater and slacks, a couple of dogs at her heels, barking and wagging their tails in greeting.

She held out her hand, 'You must be Mr Stafford,' she glanced over Larry's shoulder and hesitated a moment as she saw Kate getting out of the car, 'and . . . er . . . '

'My wife,' Larry said simply.

'Of course,' she replied quickly, 'we kept the garden room for you, let me take one of those cases.'

The inside of the house was gracious but not chintzy and whimsy, Kate felt a sudden stab of sadness as she imagined it as the private house it would never be again. The garden room proved to be what had obviously once been the morning or breakfast room. It was high ceilinged with panelled walls and french windows led into a paved garden where a few roses still bloomed in the pale winter sunshine. Somehow the big fourposter bed looked slightly incongruous in the setting, and Kate's eye slid away from it . . . but the room was warm and comfortable with big easy chairs, a wash basin, an enormous mahogany wardrobe and tallboy, which reminded Kate of her childhood, and in the wide grate, a fire of fragrant apple logs burned. 'It's lovely,' Kate said involuntarily.

The woman smiled, 'I'm afraid tea is finished, but I could get a pot sent in here if you like?'

Kate shook her head, 'No thank you very much, we won't trouble you now, we'd just like to change into something comfortable, have a wash and freshen up.'

The woman gave her a quick glance, tinged with curiosity, at least Kate thought it was. Quickly she turned away and snapped open the fasteners of her case. 'Shall I put on a dress or trousers, it doesn't look a very formal place?' she said to Larry . . . she had a sudden ridiculous reluctance to take her clothes off in front of him . . . as if he guessed what she was thinking, he said, 'I'll just pop out and see if there's a shop anywhere, grab an evening paper perhaps.' He stooped and kissed her lightly on the cheek. 'Put on whatever you like, you always look delicious to me. Just see you're still here when I get back.'

Now she unpacked and changed quickly, renewing her make-up and listening all the while for Larry's step. She put on the jersey dress with the halter neck, she was conscious it was very revealing, more daring than any dress she'd ever worn before. Tom wouldn't have liked it, for a moment she felt cheap — but it was Larry she was married to now . . . as if on cue, the door opened and he came in, a folded paper under his arm.

'There's the most beautiful copy book Cotswold village just round the corner, begging to be painted,' he smiled at her. 'Think you'll be able to stand it if I make a few sketches? It might fit into the oil series.'

She went and put her arms round his

neck, 'Of course, I'll love watching you, and I can wander along the lanes, exploring. Pity we haven't a dog, still maybe I can borrow those spaniels, they look a bit on the plump side, some exercise might be welcome.'

She could see he hadn't really taken in what she was saying, he was looking at her dress, 'Darling Kate, you look wonderful,' his eyes were full of undisguised admiration, she dropped her gaze, feeling the warmth of embarrassment creep up her neck.

'I . . . it's a bit young perhaps,' she hesitated.

She knew well enough to what he was referring, the physical attraction — was that really why she'd bought the dress? To try to prove something to herself, to stimulate him, give the impression she was his own age and generation . . . She turned away for a moment, hating the dress now, wishing she'd never bought it. One thing was certain, she'd never wear that hateful nightie. She sensed him behind her as he drew her into his arms, turning to face him, as he bent and kissed her soft skin. 'To me you're younger than spring itself Kate, age is not counted in hours and years, don't make a thing of time . . .'

The warmth of his lips brought a rush of desire and longing to her, making her cling to him for a moment. Then gently she disengaged herself, and went towards the door, holding out her hand, smiling, pleased now, if he liked the dress, then no one else's opinion mattered.

There were only two other tables in the dining room occupied — of course it was out of season, in fact it was surprising the hotel was open at all, but apparently there was fishing and hunting in the area, and also a boarding school, so that often parents used it during the term time when visiting their children. One of the couples did indeed have two young boys with them. They seemed unnaturally subdued for teenagers, their parents looked too old for them somehow. The mother looked bored and the father was slowly chewing his food as though he was having trouble with his teeth. The boys looked well scrubbed, with slicked back hair and dark suits with long trousers. They would have been much happier in jeans and tee shirts, Kate thought. She saw Larry glance at them, he adored children she knew, and she thought with a pang that even if she had a child soon, she would be older even than the mother of these two boys when they were teenagers, would she look bored, be too tired to cope with children? And yet at 41 she was not really too old to have a child . . . once again she felt a little stab of fear at what she had done, what she had taken on.

The only other couple were obviously permanent residents — retired perhaps, their table carried bottles of pills and tablets, a packet of health food, some tonic wine, and starch reduced crisp-bread.

Everyone spoke in low tones as if they were in church. Suddenly Kate wished they'd stayed at home, or perhaps taken a furnished cottage on a beach in Cornwall . . . somewhere where they could have been alone . . .

She felt Larry's eyes on her as she pushed her food round her plate, her appetite gone now . . . she knew he must be thinking that this was her second honeymoon, that she'd done all this before, was bound to be comparing it — and him — with the first-time, and Tom . . . Maybe he too was longing to be reassured, longed to ask, 'Are you sure you haven't made a mistake, sure you love me?'

Then at last they were alone. He turned out the light, and gently lifted her into his arms, carrying her to the enormous bed and laying her tenderly among the covers which smelt sweet of country air and lavender, and everything else vanished in the wonder of their love for he was all she could have wished for as a lover, and now husband;

and they lay and watched the dancing shadows on the ceiling from the dying logs in the grate, and talked, and laughed a little, and then kissed, and slept, as lovers will . . .

6

The golden days, the velvet nights, all passed like a dream. They explored the Cotswold lanes and fields and woods in the warm December sunshine, clear blue skies above, the warmth of the weather seemed to have soaked even into the honey coloured stones of the cottages and houses. Larry made some charcoal sketches, and notes of colours, while Kate walked the two dogs from the hotel. She felt a deep, fulfilled content, a happiness she wouldn't have believed possible. There had only been one jarring note . . .

She had climbed into the big bed as usual while Larry drew back the curtains and opened the windows, letting the great full moon spill its silver into the room, and she'd let her tongue slip for a moment as she said, 'Tom always managed to get into bed first and left me to open the window.' She stopped, as the words hung in mid air. Larry climbed in beside her, drawing her into his arms and saying softly, 'Don't stop Kate, you never mention Tom, why don't you? I'm not jealous, you can't be jealous of someone who . . . who isn't here any more.' She'd buried her head in the warmth of his shoulder and cried while he stroked her hair and whispered tenderly, soothing her like a child until at last she lay back, exhausted, not knowing why she cried. But it was as if the tender wraith of Tom had at last been exorcised.

'You're so kind to me, my love, why are you so kind?' she whispered.

'That's easy,' he laughed, 'Because I love you of course.'

And she was persuaded it was so.

At the end of the week she still floated on a cloud of happiness and contentment as they drove back to the Mill. They had been wonderful days of sunshine and love, and now she looked forward to seeing Roz, to being home again, to picking up the threads of living, and to Christmas.

The day had clouded over and it was cold and windy as they went up the drive. A shiny new car stood in front of the house. 'What a beaut!' Larry whistled, 'wonder who's that is? One day I hope I'll be able to afford one like it.'

Kate put her hand on his arm, 'You won't have to wait for one day, it's yours, my wedding present. I asked them to deliver it today so it would be waiting for you, and I also asked them to take that disreputable wreck of yours away to the scrap yard!'

For a moment before he spoke a little frown of annoyance furrowed his brow — he wasn't used to having things done for him in quite such a sweeping manner, he would like to have seen to the disposal of Fred himself . . . but he turned a smile on Kate. 'You wonderful woman, but you had no right to spend all that money,' he paused a moment and then laughed, 'What a pair we are!

Were you wondering why I hadn't given you something for a wedding present.'

She shook her head, 'I hadn't thought about it . . . after all . . . ' she bit back the words, 'after all it's not like a first wedding, when one is setting up house . . . '

But he went on without apparently noticing, 'In a moment you'll have to think about it, that is if everything has gone according to plan between Roz and me . . . '

She was about to ask him what he meant, when the front door burst open and a bundle of pale gold fur tumbled out, followed by Roz with a collar and a piece of chewed lead in her hand. She waved to them, and tried to recapture the puppy who was leaping about and barking in a fenzy of welcome and delight. Kate managed at last to catch hold of the wriggling body . . . 'What on earth?'

'Fred the second,' Larry laughed at her, 'my present for you. I hadn't thought of the name before, but now there's no original Fred, it would be a good idea if this bundle of mischief replaced him — my wedding present my love, I hope he brings you a lot of happiness.'

Roz stood watching them as Kate bent down to caress the puppy who had rolled over on his back, exposing a pale pink stomach to be scratched. Larry was laughing at her — they both looked young happy and in love . . . Larry smiled at Roz now. 'Well the happy couple are safely home from the wilds of Gloucestershire.'

She tried to answer his grin, but Kate noticed she looked more tired than ever, although she had promised to have a good rest while they were away. Kate had kept on Jessie from the village, who had always worked for her since Roz was little, mostly she did the cleaning, but she was an excellent cook too, so there had really been nothing for Roz to do, but she looked worn out.

'It's no good,' Kate murmured to Larry later when they were in the bedroom, 'I'll just have to try and get out of her what the trouble is — I know she's in love with Dick, and he's married, but it shouldn't make her ill like this, she'll have some kind of breakdown if it goes on.'

It seemed strange to have Larry about the house all the time — and with the right to her bedroom too, the room she and Tom had shared, it still gave her an odd feeling of guilt. But Larry showed such tenderness, such an unspoken acknowledgement of the privacy to which she had been used, that it all helped to make their love seem natural, easy and right.

Now her days were full and blissful. Fred was a bundle of energy and had to be house trained, and persuaded to sleep in the kitchen. He howled all through the first night, and the second, so that in the end Kate couldn't bear to hear him and buried her head under the bedclothes, so that at last Larry went down and brought the wriggling bundle and put him in his basket on the floor, where he stayed for one minute flat, and then was pushing at Kate's face, his huge paws on the bed. They laughed, and heaved him up on the eiderdown, where at last, having turned round three times, he settled down with a little sigh of satisfaction.

'Poor baby,' Kate said, 'I guess he was lonely, missing his Mum,' and Larry said, 'I can quite understand how he feels poor chap, both of us are lucky we're not alone any more.'

All that spoiled the serenity of her life was Roz and her unhappiness, until at last one afternoon when Larry had gone to replenish his store of paints and canvasses in Kingsford, she made the girl sit down in the kitchen where she was making pastry for supper, 'Look, I know there's something wrong, something more serious than just being hopelessly in love, can't you tell me?' she said gently.

For a moment she thought Roz was going to get up and dash out of the kitchen, but she said slowly, not looking at her mother, 'There is. I'm pregnant, and the trouble is the baby won't have a father.' Then she put her head down on her hands and burst into tears as Kate stood with her hand on her mouth, speechless, helpless . . . then as she saw the sobs that seemed to be tearing Roz's thin body apart, she ran over and put her arms round her.

'My poor love, my baby, why didn't you tell me? Keeping it all to yourself. This wretched pride of yours . . . How on earth long have you known?'

Roz lifted her swollen, tear stained face to her mother, 'It's due in May — I tried to tell you when I came home, that first time, I was pretty certain then, when you and Larry . . . but when I saw how things were between you — and then the wedding and everything, I just couldn't spoil your happiness.'

For a moment Kate felt choked with unshed tears, thinking of what Roz must have suffered, watching herself and Larry in their fulfilled happiness — how lost and lonely she must have been, just as she had felt as a child when she thought Kate was going to have another baby — no wonder she looked like she did.

'I thought perhaps being on our own in America — when I told him about the baby, it might make a difference,' Roz went on, her voice still broken with sobs, 'but he just didn't want to know. He said some awful things, things I couldn't even tell you . . . I thought, as he always said he liked kids, wanted a family, it might be what he needed, but he told me if his wife divorced him he'd have nothing — it's her money behind the stables — he just can't afford to leave her.'

'But doesn't she know about you, about the baby?'

Roz nodded, 'Oh yes, I'm not the first by any means, but she always turns a blind eye, she doesn't care so long as he stays married to her, you see she's a lot older than him, and not very pretty.' Suddenly she realized what she'd said, quickly she put out her hand and touched Kate's arm, 'Oh Mum, I didn't mean that, I spoke without thinking,' sobs shook her again, 'honestly half the time I don't know what I am doing or saying . . . you and Larry are quite different.'

'Well what does he suggest?' Kate went on slowly, her arm round Roz, 'I mean surely he realizes he's responsible for his own child, however foolish you may have been?'

Roz gave a mirthless laugh, 'He had a wonderful suggestion, in fact I had a feeling it wasn't the first time he'd been in exactly the same situation, it came out so pat, that I had an abortion. But I never will,' she said vehemently, 'In any case it's too late now. And that was another thing he accused me of, not telling him about it till it was too late, but he was generous enough to say I could stay on at the stables till I couldn't work any longer, and that he'd pay all my expenses . . . I shall just have to get the baby adopted, that's all.' She paused, 'so I'm going back after

Christmas, till April anyway,' she faltered. 'I'm still wondering, hoping, that when he sees the baby things may be different. He isn't really bad, Mum, it's just that he's weak, without her money he couldn't exist, he told me that. He never really loved her, but he likes the good things in life — fast cars and horses, nice clothes.'

'And pretty girls,' Kate said quickly, turning away so Roz shouldn't see the expression in her eyes. If she'd had Fordyce there at the moment, she'd gladly have rung his neck, she could understand only too well a mother killing to protect her young from harm, whether mental or physical . . . but she said, 'Must you go back, won't you stay here, and have the baby, then decide about the future? You know Larry and I would love to have you.'

Roz smiled, 'Thanks Mum, but no all the same. For one thing I'm a big girl now, I must stand on my own feet, and after all I knew what I was doing when we became lovers. It all seemed so wonderful, so right at the time,' she paused, 'anyway I wouldn't want to play gooseberry on you two love birds, it would hardly be the best way to start married life.' She sounded suddenly so old and wise that Kate felt almost her junior. 'And it would hardly be fair on Larry to have a pregnant step-daughter hung round his neck.'

'This is still your home, as well as ours,' Kate said quickly. But there was no changing Roz's mind.

Although Kate was far from happy about the situation, at least the air was cleared, but even though Larry had tried to persuade her to stay at home, give up her job, she held grimly to her decision to go back to work as soon as Christmas was over.

'I just have to have final proof . . . when the baby's born,' she said, and he'd put his arm round the thin shoulders and drawn her to him, as he said, 'I do understand — you must do as you think best.'

Kate and Larry were like two

children now as they prepared for Christmas. They drove out into lanes and Larry climbed a tree to cut holly, Fred stood at the foot of the tree barking his head off, certain his master had gone quite mad, only cats climbed trees. They piled the branches, heavy with rich, shining scarlet berries, into the back of the car, they found a bunch of mistletoe growing in one of the old apple trees in the orchard at the mill, both Kate and Roz swore they'd never seen any there before, 'It's witchcraft,' they laughed at Larry, and he drew Kate into the circle of his arm and kissed her cold, rosy cheek. 'Each kiss under the bunch means one berry must be taken off,' he laughed, holding it above her head with his other hand, 'so it's bad luck on the last arrivals.'

Kate and Roz spent hours in the kitchen making mincemeat and puddings, the first time she'd done so since Tom's death, a turkey had been promised from a local farm, and Fred had to be kept out of everything that it was possible for a lively puppy to get itself into. 'By the size of his paws, he's going to be the biggest labrador ever born,' Kate laughed one day as she dried muddy marks off the kitchen floor.

'And if his appetite's anything to go by, he's going to end up as a lion and not a dog!' Roz exclaimed. Temporarily she seemed happier, and had put on a little weight, although the baby didn't show yet, but Kate dreaded to think what would happen when she went back to the stables, she was sure she'd starve herself, sink back into the misery that had engulfed her. But she knew it was hopeless to try and persuade her against her will, she would have to work out her own problems, live her own life with the best will in the world that was something no mother could protect her child from.

A sparkling rime of snow and frost gilded the trees and grass, so the old Mill looked like the traditional Christmas card. Larry mulled wine, and Kate couldn't help the great burst of joy inside her as they sat round the huge log fire, drinking it. This was all she had longed for, a complete family. She was sure that wherever Tom was, he'd approve, for many times they'd discussed what they should do if one of them should die when they were still fairly young, and leave the other behind.

'It's not morbid,' Kate had said when Tom protested, 'just sensible. I'd like you to find someone nice to look after you, I couldn't bear to think of you lonely and on your own,' and Tom had laughed and said, 'We've got years yet love, you might even fancy some other chap before that,' and she'd put her arms round him and closed his mouth with kisses, never dreaming that time would be so short before the idea became reality.

And then Christmas was over, and Roz got ready to leave again. Before she went she clung to her mother and Kate said once more, 'Please come home at least to have the baby . . . ' but she shook her head.

'No Mum, I've made up my mind, I must do it my way, after all, you did your own thing, marrying Larry.'

'I know,' Kate said softly, 'and you don't think I was wrong do you? Ten years is an awful lot of time.'

Roz shook her head, 'I've never been able to see what age has to do with it, you've so much in common, and somehow Larry seems older than 30, and after all you're a very young 41.'

Kate sighed, 'I hope you're right, sometimes — oh I don't know, I think perhaps it isn't fair on him.'

Roz put her arms round her, 'Now who's being silly? It's obvious he adores you,' she drew away, 'as a matter of fact it makes me horribly jealous.'

Then quickly she ran down the stairs, calling over her shoulder, 'See you, and give my love to Larry.'

Kate ran after her, a tissue wrapped parcel in her hand. 'Look love, here's a nightie I bought in a moment of

. . . well weakness I suppose really. I'll never wear it, it's black lace, a bit old for you, but definitely too young for me.'

Roz unwrapped the parcel, gasping with pleasure when she saw the lace and fur, 'You silly old thing, what made you lose your nerve and chicken out? I bet Larry would have loved you in it.' She kissed Kate, 'but thanks all the same, it's nice to have a bit of glam. When you're in my condition.'

Kate lifted a couple of the cases, 'Do be careful, you really shouldn't carry heavy things.'

Roz laughed, 'Not to worry, I'm as strong as the horses in the stables, and I'll fix up a Mother and Baby Home in plenty of time, so don't fuss,' she dropped her eyes for a moment, 'then if Dick still feels the same, well I'll just get the baby adopted.'

It all sounded terribly clinical and unfeeling to Kate, as if the baby were to be made into some kind of commercial commodity . . . but she had to let Roz go and she turned back into the house feeling bereft, as the little scarlet car disappeared down the drive, she and Roz had never been so close as during the last few days.

Fred was howling to be let out of the kitchen and she clipped on his lead and took him to the woods to look for Larry who was collecting kindling wood. Suddenly she felt drained of all energy as if Roz had taken some of her life with her. Quickly she pulled herself together, she mustn't let Larry see her lassitude. He was always so full of boundless life and energy, so vital, so alive.

And so the days took a kind of pattern — Larry painted most of the day while the light remained — he used the old store room where they'd held the exhibition, as a studio now, and he was completing the last of the paintings for the oil company. Kate was certain they were the best things he'd ever done.

Their evenings in front of the log fire were one of the best parts of the day, sometimes he'd read to her, he had a beautiful accentless voice. Kate had remarked on this one day for she knew he'd been brought up in the Midlands.

'I expect it's because I was reared in a convent, nuns seem classless, and mostly without any kind of accent either, as far as I remember anyway,' he grinned, 'but as long as I please you my love, that's all that matters.'

Sometimes they listened to music, then at half past ten they'd take Fred for his last run up the lane, whatever the weather, running back laughing, in old duffle coats if it was raining, standing arms entwined, to point out to each other the different stars in the clear, frosty sky, when the nights were dry and bright.

Life was perfect, apart from the ever present worry about Roz.

She wrote occasionally, although she had never been a very good letter writer. She'd got fixed up in a Mother and Baby Home near London, one of the best, Dick was paying all the expenses . . . she would be going there in April when she couldn't work any longer . . . as soon as the baby was born — if necessary she'd have it adopted, then she hoped to be able to go back to work, whether at the same stables she hadn't made up her mind, so much would depend on Dick . . . 'But don't worry Mum, I've never felt so well, so don't flap. I'll let you know when it's all over.'

Kate had difficulty in suppressing an almost overwhelming desire to write to Dick Fordyce and give him a piece of her mind, but Larry persuaded her it would do no one any good, least of all Roz. Apart from this one worry, there were times when in her great happiness she felt a stab of disloyalty as she remembered Tom . . . the curious part was that in spite of the fact that she'd always had the feeling their marriage had been perfect, now she realized that the relationship she had with Larry was something so different, so much more fulfilling, that in a way she hadn't even known what the word love meant, nor the living of life as it should be.

Larry too seemed happy as far as she could tell, it was a relief not to have to spend his day teaching when he was longing to do his own work, he had a full quota of commissions, the 'Oil Mogul' paintings had been a great success and brought the offers of work rolling in. He arranged sittings for those who wanted portraits done at the Mill Studio, sometimes he went to people's houses if they were important enough, and demanded it! But he much preferred to work at home in the right atmosphere.

And so the days and weeks melted into months and April lived up to its traditional beauty with bird song and dancing daffodils, bursting pink blossom and the heady perfume of flowers on the soft breeze. Kate thought of Roz and knew her time was near . . . it was a couple of weeks since she'd heard from her. The girl had deliberately not given her the name of the Home because she knew her mother would fuss, but now Kate wished at least she had the phone number.

Fred had grown and fulfilled the promise of being a big dog, but he was so gentle and loving that Kate wondered how they had ever thought of the mill as a home without him.

Now as she sat shelling broad beans she saw him lift his head as if he heard something she could not, his tail started to thump on the floor as a car turned into the gate. Kate got up and went to the front door. A scarlet Mini . . . her heart missed a beat. Roz's hand waved from the window as the car drew up. For a moment she hesitated, wondering how things would be — how Roz would be, what had happened to the baby . . .

She wasn't left long in doubt. Roz threw open the door, Kate heard a soft sound from the back seat of the car. She glanced through the window and saw a carrycot, a small fist waved in the air and a tuft of ginger hair stuck up above the blankets. For a moment she couldn't believe her eyes, then she felt Roz's arms round her as the girl buried her face in Kate's neck, 'Oh Mum, I don't know what you're going to say, I don't even know what to think myself. I've kept him. Young Tom. I named him after Dad. It was . . . I couldn't give him up when I heard him cry . . . ' Her body felt so thin under the shirt and jeans, and it was torn now by sobs as though she would never be able to stop. 'I've been such an idiot.' Gently Kate disengaged herself.

'Let's take him inside, he's probably hungry, and very damp if you've driven all the way from Kent, and I just can't wait to see my grandson. Larry'll be over the moon, as they say.'

It was only as she lifted the carrycot out of the car that the true realization of the words hit her, that this was indeed her grandson, flesh of her flesh, hers and Tom's.

Roz gave her a quick look, 'Do you honestly think he won't mind?'

They both turned as they heard a

step on the gravel behind them and Larry held out his arms to Roz. 'What won't Larry mind?' he smiled at her, 'Having a ready made step grandson? Let's take him inside and have a look at the young fella.'

He took the carrycot from Kate as she gazed down at the unfocused blue eyes, which somehow even now reminded her of Tom, and she prayed silently, 'Thank you God, and please let everything be all right now with Roz and her son.'

It was a wonderful long, hot, golden summer, just like the one when she had met Larry. Kate couldn't remember ever having been so happy, so content. Roz was a different person, and their relationship was on a perfect footing. Now that Larry was even more and more absorbed in his work, to Kate the baby was a constant joy. Each day he grew more like Tom, watching Roz with the baby as he lay naked on the lawn in the hot sunshine, she felt envy as the girl said, 'Have you and Larry thought about kids, Mum? After all you're still young enough, and he'd make a marvellous father. Look how he adores young Tom.'

'We've discussed it often, Larry adores kids and he ought to have a family. I sometimes feel I'm failing him in this, but I suppose it is still early days as far as our marriage is concerned,' Kate paused, 'but not as far as my age is concerned.'

Sometimes she did feel time was running out on her, although Dr Clarke assured her there was no reason why she shouldn't become pregnant. And so she kept hoping and longing.

Meanwhile Roz said, 'I shall have to think about getting another job, I can't live off you and Larry for ever.'

Kate said nothing, but she felt a burden lifted from her heart that at least Roz had decided not to go back to Dick? Maybe at last all that was a closed chapter in her life, inevitably it couldn't be completely wiped out for young Tom was there as a constant reminder, but he was at least something good which had come out of the relationship.

Roz had told her, slowly, painfully, bit by bit, that Dick had refused even to come to the Home to see the baby, she had written and told him it was a boy, and that she was not going to have him adopted, but he hadn't answered her letter. 'I think perhaps he didn't dare let himself see the baby in case he got emotionally involved,' she added.

'Why don't you get a job locally, then I can keep an eye on young Tom during the day — that is if you must just yet, you know we love to have you both just as things are.'

Roz smiled, 'I know, that's exactly why I must try to find some kind of independence again, after all there aren't many men about who'll want to take on someone else's child,' she paused and looked away from Kate's gaze for a moment, 'I expect you'll think I'm crazy, but I don't know if I'll ever find anyone like Dick again, whatever he did, I still love him. It's just one of those things.'

Kate put her arm round her. 'In that case let's see what we can find for you, there should be plenty of scope in the district with riding stables, training establishments and so on, and anyone with your experience won't have much trouble getting fixed up.'

Roz smiled at her, 'Good, that's settled then, but if Tom's going to be a nuisance or a tie, then I'll take him to Nursery School, or find a girl from the village who could look after him for part of the day anyway.'

'Let's give it a try, I can't imagine letting anyone else take charge of my precious grandson at the moment,' Kate grinned.

Summer once again seemed reluctant to give way even to the mildness of autumn, and Kate found it hard to realize she and Larry had been married nearly a year. Roz had got a teaching job in a local riding stable which involved taking parties trekking across the moors, and she'd developed a warm tan and filled out. 'I wouldn't know she was the same person,' Kate said joyfully to Larry, 'just to think a small bundle like Tom could change a person so completely,' she pointed to where the baby was kicking and gurgling in his pram, with Fred lying, nose on paws, guarding the baby. Far from being jealous of the new addition to the family as Kate had feared, he'd taken charge completely like a silky guardian angel.

Although Kate was overjoyed that Larry's painting was now such a success, it meant she saw less and less of him, and he seemed often to be a bit short tempered, once he'd even snapped at Fred when he jumped up and knocked some paints out of his hand.

'Down, you damned dog, always under my feet!'

Kate glanced at him quickly, 'He's only pleased to see you after you've been out all day — just as I am,' she added quietly.

‘Sorry love,’ he said quickly, putting his arm round her, ‘but we did know if I was to earn my living this way, it would mean I had to be away quite a bit.’ He ran one hand through his hair. ‘It’s this portrait I’m working on, somehow I can’t get it right, I’ve spent more time and turps on it than paint.’

Kate wrinkled her brows, she couldn’t always remember exactly who he was painting, unless they came to the house. ‘Is this the one of Stephanie Welford?’

He turned from her and nodded, ‘Yes, she’s the daughter of Councillor Welford, could be a useful contact . . . they insisted I do it at their place, that may be partly the trouble.’

Kate remembered seeing the girl once, she was strikingly beautiful and when Larry had been asked to do the portrait she had imagined he would find it simple and enjoyable.

‘What’s the trouble, won’t she sit still?’ she grinned, trying to lighten his mood.

To her surprise he turned away once

more, abruptly. 'It's not funny Kate, I'm . . . oh I don't know, it's something to do with the expression in her eyes, she's so young and fresh, it's almost impossible to capture it . . . it's difficult to explain to someone who doesn't know much about painting.'

Suddenly Kate shivered as if something had walked over her grave, and a cold hand of fear clutched at her heart.

It was the first time since their marriage that for a moment she had felt shut out from Larry's work — from part of his life even.

7

Looking back later, Kate couldn't pin-point the exact moment that she was certain Larry was in love with Stephanie Welford — there were so many little things that happened almost every day which made her feel something was not right, not as it had been. Their love-making, which had been so perfect, seemed different, restrained, almost as if it were an effort for him, as though he were preoccupied so that, ever vulnerable, she drew away, and that made him angry.

At breakfast one morning she said, 'I wish you'd do a painting of young Tom, Larry. It'd be lovely to have a record of how he looks as a tiny baby — and then perhaps as a toddler — much nicer than photos.'

He'd got up abruptly, stepping on Fred's tail, impatience in his manner,

'For heaven's sake Kate! I can't spend my time painting various members of the family, I need to be paid, I'm not some kind of philanthropic society, it's a job just like any other . . . ' He'd gone out banging the door, waking young Tom, and not even stopping to comfort the dog who had yelped with pain.

For a moment Kate sat looking into space. Tom had started to coo in his carrycot, Roz had left for the stables, and suddenly she felt terribly alone. The tears started behind her eyelids, she brushed them away impatiently, self-pity was a form of indulgence she had no time for. But now as she thought back to the immediate past, there had been a change in Larry . . . she got up and went into the drawing room where the portrait he'd done of her hung over the fireplace.

She stood looking at it for a long time — but now in a new light. She looked so young, so happy then — was the mood he'd caught just wishful thinking on Larry's part she wondered. She had thought then that if only they could be together always, life must be perfect — but had that very togetherness spoilt everything? Did Larry realize now what he had missed, marrying a woman so much older? He had told her often that he'd not had much love as a child — 'Oh the nuns were kind enough in their fashion,' he'd grinned, 'we didn't exactly want for anything, it's just that nothing was ever our very own, even our clothes had been passed down — we had no one to identify with it seemed,' he'd bent and kissed her, 'not till you my darling Kate.'

Now she closed her eyes in a kind of agony, remembering. Then he had painted for the very love of it, was he changing now that work had become something by which he earned his bread and butter? A kind of driving anxiety not to be beholden to her.

She went back into the kitchen and started to wash up.

That evening after supper Larry said, 'By the way, I shall be using the studio for the next few days, the Welfords are having their house done up, some party or other they're giving, so it means there's nowhere quiet to paint.'

Kate glanced at him, but he had the evening paper in front of his face. 'I see, that means Miss Welford will be coming here.'

He grunted.

'I'd better tidy the room up a bit, it looks as if a hurricane has hit it,' she said lightly.

He rustled the pages as he turned over, 'No need to bother, no one expects an artist to be tidy,' he said drily.

Perhaps it was seeing them together, and because she loved him so much — maybe it was because now he never talked about the portrait he was doing as he usually did, for where he was concerned her heart was as sensitive as a butterfly's antenna.

Kate was always meticulously careful not to intrude on any painting sessions Larry had at the Mill — usually at a pre-arranged time she would take in a tray of coffee, both model and painter had to have a break at some time, usually she didn't stay to drink a cup with them. On the first morning of Stephanie's sitting she knocked and walked in. She was chatting away and Larry seemed to be listening — unlike his usual manner, for most often he lent a very unwilling ear to chatter — anxious to be back again at his canvas before the magic mood should be lost . . . in fact they were quite engrossed in conversation. Larry had turned away abruptly, pretending to be absorbed in cleaning his brushes.

She poured the coffee — Larry turned round, 'Oh Kate, this is Miss Welford — Kate, my wife.' Kate smiled at her.

'Please call me Stevie — everyone does, you don't usually sound so formal, Larry.' She glanced at him under the curve of her lashes.

There was no doubt she was very beautiful — and very young. All Kate's doubts and fears, which she had tried to ignore — came rushing back. Her throat felt tight as she handed the cup to Stevie.

'I understand from my husband you've recently left school, have you made plans for your future?' As she said the words they sounded stilted. She had only meant to try to make polite conversation, not to let the awkward silence hang in the air between the three of them in case the girl sensed some kind of atmosphere. She had a feeling the candid blue eyes could see through her, pierce her fragile armour.

'Oh something with kids I think, I just adore them. I do some part time work now in the local Orphanage,' she smiled at Kate, 'Mind you, don't imagine that I think kids are all innocent little dears, some of them are complete horrors, and would stop at nothing.' She bit into a chocolate biscuit with even, white teeth, 'but as matron says, it's all a part of the rich fabric of life,' she grinned at Kate, 'anyway when I get married I'm going to have dozens of children.'

'You'll need a husband with plenty of money,' Kate said drily.

'Oh I don't know, Daddy's loaded,' she said with such disarming candour that Kate had to laugh. Larry sat in the window seat, not joining in now with the conversation. Kate couldn't bring herself to look at him for some reason, couldn't risk meeting his eyes.

'Well, I must leave you to get on with the portrait,' Kate glanced at the nearly finished picture. All the youth and joy of a young girl shone from the eyes.

'Thanks for the coffee Kate, and before I go, can I see your grandson? I passed the pram in the garden, but I didn't like to look in case I woke him.'

'Of course, call me, I'll be in the kitchen,' Kate said. She went out, closing the door softly, for a moment she stood in the hall, her hands holding the tray shook so much that some of the milk spilt. Had she imagined it or had the girl deliberately emphasized the fact that Tom was her grandson? It made her sound as old as the hills, generations away from herself — and Larry.

* * *

Larry had finished the portrait. He had told her the Welfords were giving a party, and had asked him and Kate.

'It seems they're very pleased and as they are having a silver wedding party, which happens to coincide with the portrait being finished, its a kind of celebration,' he hesitated. 'It could be quite a good bit of publicity, he knows everyone who's anyone round here.'

He wants to go — to see her again — Kate thought, anything to be near her. For a moment she was tempted to tell him to go alone, but quickly she checked herself. If there was something between him and Stevie, then she'd fight it to the bitter end.

'I'd like that,' she said lightly, 'it's ages since we went out, I'll buy myself a new dress, get my hair done.'

For a moment his eyes met hers, for a moment he looked like the old Larry as he said, 'Don't buy a new one, wear that one you wore on our honeymoon.'

The halter neck — the clinging jersey — so he remembered. She had a feeling that at a party like the Welfords would give she'd look like mutton dressed as lamb, she could imagine the tongues wagging as she stood by Larry — 'Nearly old enough to be his mother.' 'Wearing a dress like that, showing so much bare flesh — disgusting!'

It had been all right when they were at the hotel, where no one knew them, but she didn't feel she could face the people who knew her, had known her when she was married to Tom. She'd buy something with a high neck and sleeves. No I won't! she thought defiantly, I'll have my hair styled, get some fresh make-up, Roz'll help me — and I'll wear that dress.

But as the party night drew near, she seemed to feel more and more exhausted and depressed, she wished now she'd said she wouldn't go, but she had no valid excuse. Bitterly she thought, I really have no ties, no responsibilities, no child of my own who can't be left. I haven't even been able to fulfil the most elementary function of a wife, and give my husband a child . . . she was surprised even at herself. Never had she felt like this before. Maybe both she and Larry had been working too hard — she looking after young Tom, although that was a delight, and she knew she only had to speak the word and Roz would get a girl to look after him. She didn't want that. But perhaps they needed a holiday — the one they'd promised themselves, the extra honeymoon they'd planned, and never got around to. Maybe they needed to be alone without all the outside pressures which seemed to surround them.

On top of everything else, she'd been having odd sensations like pins and needles in her hands and arms, sometimes they were almost numb, and a pain would shoot up the nerves, making her catch her breath.

'Just rheumatism,' she told herself. She'd always been so healthy, never fussed about herself, she tried to ignore the symptoms — but Roz noticed the dark shadows under eyes, and how thin she'd got.

'Mum you must take things a bit more easily, you're looking really peaky. I shall get Doctor Clarke to come and run the rule over you.'

'Nonsense!' Kate forced a smile. It had been one of her depressed days, when to her Larry seemed far away. 'It's been a hot summer, maybe it's got me down a bit.' She would like to have confided her doubts and worries to Roz, but somehow she couldn't bring herself to start . . . she told herself she didn't want to spoil Roz's new found peace of mind — but in her heart she knew it was pride kept her silent.

The party was in full swing when they arrived. The Welfords were a delightful couple and their evident delight in the portrait of their daughter, and admiration for Larry, made Kate feel better — maybe the whole thing had been in her imagination after all.

Mrs Welford took Larry's arm and drew him into the big drawing room while Kate went on up the stairs to the room she had pointed out, to leave her coat and comb her hair. In the mirror her face gazed back at her, the eyes looked enormous in the pale face, there were violet shadows in the hollows — 'I look every day of my age,' she thought bitterly, 'no wonder Roz thinks I ought to see the doctor.'

Back downstairs she watched Larry as he moved among the guests, bowing his head as he listened to one and another, then throwing back his head as he laughed at some remark.

'How young he looks,' she thought wistfully, and it didn't escape her notice that Stephanie's eyes too were following him, nor was there any mistaking the emotion on her mobile face, any more than in the picture Larry had painted.

Suddenly the noise, the music, and the tinkle of glasses smote upon her like a physical blow. Her eyes felt dazzled by the lights and the gay dresses, and sparkling jewellery all around her. It was like being in the centre of some kind of never ending pattern, and yet not part of it.

At that moment Claude Welford took the champagne glass she was clasping automatically, 'Now Mrs Stafford, we can't have you hugging a lukewarm drop of wine like that! Let me fill it up for you!' She smiled at him as he took her arm, and led her to the long table which was serving as bar and buffet. The champagne was good, as were the snacks and sandwiches, and she knew there was really no reason why she shouldn't enjoy herself. It was just a kind of unease that filled her, and an awful overpowering tiredness.

The October evening was mild as summer, the french windows opened on to the lawn, and some of the guests had wandered into the garden where the perfume of late roses still hung on the warm air.

Kate sank gratefully on to a swing hammock with a canvas cover which had been placed just below the terrace. There she was hidden in a little world of her own, she lent her head back and closed her eyes.

Then she heard voices just above her. She looked up. Stevie was leaning against the stone balustrade of the terrace, silhouetted against the lights streaming from the windows, was the head and shoulders of a man. Kate knew she should move, she had no intention of eavesdropping, but even as she put down her hand to push herself up from the seat, she realized it was Larry . . . and as she watched, frozen into immobility, the feeling as if it were all some awful nightmare, flooded through her as the girl stood on tiptoe and reached up to kiss Larry.

Kate closed her eyes, imagining his arms round her, the trembling of the slight body, the perfume of her hair . . . there was no sound. She opened her eyes — they'd gone. For a moment she felt dizzy, faint even, unconsciously she had twisted the champagne glass in her hand and broken the stem. Little scarlet drops of blood spattered the skirt of her dress. Now it was as if she'd imagined the whole scene, like an act in a play at which she had been the sole member of the audience. Anger, sorrow, humiliation, filled her in turn.

Somehow she got to her feet, and stumbling through the dew drenched grass, made her way to where Larry had parked the car. Thankfully she found it unlocked, and she sank down in the passenger seat as sobs wrenched her body, and tears poured down her cheeks as though they would never stop.

There was a clean duster in the pocket of the car and at last she wiped her face as she became calmer, somehow she would have to patch up her make-up, go back and fetch her coat, make her apologies and say she had a headache . . . but for a moment she had to sit and pull herself together.

It was true then — Larry and Stevie were in love. She had to face that fact, whatever she might plan to do.

She hadn't really thought of Stevie as grown up till now . . . in some ways she'd seemed quite childish that day at the mill . . . but she was probably only a few years younger than Larry . . . in some subtle way she had grown to think of him as her own generation — it had been such a gradual process she hadn't noticed — in some ways he had perhaps gravitated to her outlook, although sometimes she had been pulled up short when she'd been remembering something — an old dance tune perhaps, which he couldn't recall, and then she'd realize with a shock she'd been almost eleven when he was born — and suddenly now she realized he'd lost a whole decade from his life, being with her . . . and thinking of Stevie, listening to her talking, probably he had realized what he'd missed, maybe he felt there was an abyss of wasted years at his feet, years which he could never recapture, for the simple reason that he had never lived them.

She had become a little more composed now, she got out her compact and powdered her nose, put on fresh lipstick, combed her hair. One or two people were coming out to the cars, the party must be breaking up. She didn't think somehow that anyone would have missed her.

8

They didn't talk much as they drove home. Larry seemed elated, he'd had several useful introductions. He didn't appear to notice that Kate answered in monosyllables. Her heart and her head ached, she knew she couldn't wait till the morning to challenge him about his feelings for Stevie — ask him what he planned to do. She had to know.

She went slowly up the stairs while he put the car away, took off the low cut dress — she'd never wear that again she was sure — she unpinned her hair and put on her dressing gown. As he opened the bedroom door his eyes met hers in the mirror . . . his were troubled, almost like the eyes of a child who has been hurt in some way it doesn't understand — but it was no good, she lifted her head and said, 'Are you in love with Stephanie, Larry? I have to know, but before you answer, I must tell you that I saw you kissing on the terrace — I had no intention of spying.'

For a moment he stood absolutely still looking at her. She longed to turn round, to draw his head to her breast, to say, 'Tell me it isn't true — tell me I was mistaken, it wasn't really you.'

But he turned away with a gesture of despair almost. 'My dear Kate, it wasn't what you think, I wasn't kissing her — she kissed me — that's quite a different thing as you must know, it was just an impulsive gesture by a young girl — she was excited and pleased at the success of the painting — that's all.'

Kate didn't answer, seeking a reply, feeling helplessly inarticulate. As if he took her silence for reproach, he burst out, 'You're regretting marrying me, aren't you Kate? I suppose I've been aware of it for some time. Maybe if Roz had been at home when we met, it would never have happened.'

She stared at him in amazement, 'But

Roz has nothing to do with it, how can you say that?'

'I'm not saying Roz had anything directly to do with our getting married, what I mean is you had no one here to love — no one to care about, and you are full of love Kate, it has to be spent on someone. If you'd had Roz, and young Tom, you wouldn't have been so vulnerable, so ready to find an object to love . . . it just happened that I came along at the right moment.'

She got to her feet, 'That's not true! Whenever I'd met you, under whatever circumstances, I'd have fallen in love with you. It's cruel to talk like that.'

Now he faced her, white, his eyes blazing. 'So what it comes to is the fact that you don't trust me — you think I'm having an affair with a young girl, and your pride's hurt, is that it?'

She felt helpless, she put out her hands, but he ignored her and she dropped them to her sides in a gesture of surrender.

'If you really want to know, Stephanie

Welford has been a pest — I wish I'd never taken on the commission, but I thought it might lead to further work, which it has done actually. What I didn't realize was the kind of girl she is,' he paused. 'I'd met her ages ago, not at the Grammar School, through a friend of hers who was one of my pupils — a girl called Kathie Fry. It seems she had some kind of silly crush on me — you know what girls are at that age — very impressionable. And Kathie was always talking to Stevie about me during the holidays, when she was home from boarding school.'

As he spoke Kate could imagine it — two schoolgirls together, giggling, discussing the dishy art master — Larry says this, Larry says that . . . his voice was going on.

'Apparently Stevie told her friend to belt up, she was sick of my name, then we met at one of those ghastly old girls' parties these schools have, long before I knew you. I took her out a couple of times, I suppose I was silly enough to be flattered by her admiration, or whatever, but there was nothing in it, I swear it to you Kate.'

She stood looking at the moon drenched garden, hearing his voice, but her heart would not let her believe him — all the time he had been in love with a younger girl — it must have been her money after all, like her friends had warned her . . .

' . . . and then she came and asked me to do this portrait — I thought it was her parents who had commissioned it, but apparently it was her own idea, a silver wedding present for them. I couldn't see any harm in it . . . ' he hesitated, 'the money was too good to refuse — you must realize that Kate.'

'And the chance to be near her,' she thought bitterly, as she swung round now to face him. 'Why didn't you tell me from the beginning that you already knew her? You never told me you'd even met.'

He gave a gesture of despair, 'You never asked me, I didn't think you were all that interested,' he paused, 'as a matter of fact these days you're always tired, or tied up with the baby — or just about to take the dog out . . . there's never any time for me — it hasn't worked out has it Kate?'

She wanted to believe all he told her, but he had deceived her, that she couldn't forgive.

'I suppose it's because I don't seem able to have a child,' she said, 'I know you want a family, a young girl would be able to give you a baby — and plenty of money,' she added, 'it's not my fault — and as for young Tom, I thought you were pleased for him to be here — I didn't realize you resented him.'

He sank down on the bed, his head in his hands, 'Oh my God, Kate, we can't go on like this, we shall tear each other apart.'

'Then if that's what you want,' she said sharply, 'not to go on . . . ' holding back the tears which pricked her eyelids, determined he shouldn't see her cry . . . but directly she'd said the words she could have bitten out her tongue . . . however pride wouldn't let her take them back.

He got to his feet. As if she were rooted to the spot she watched as he got a case from the cupboard and threw his night things into it, snapping the locks shut. She couldn't really believe it was happening — it was as if some power beyond her control, motivated her, put words into her mouth. A feeling of utter helplessness filled her as without another word he went out, banging the door behind him. She took a few steps forward, her hand outstretched, his name frozen on her lips . . . there was a sudden tingling up her arms, and then nothing . . . just a numbness as though she literally had no arms, no hands.

She wasn't conscious that the thin drawn out scream came from her throat as Roz, clad only in her nightgown, rushed into the bedroom to find her mother sitting like a doll with all the stuffing gone, her arms hanging loosely by her sides, the tears running unchecked down her cheeks as she gasped out the words — 'Roz — get the doctor quickly — I'm paralysed.'

* * *

Kate lay in a private side ward at the little hospital in Kingsford. Originally it had been a Cottage Hospital, and because of a local petition, it had been allowed to remain, a kind of backwater from the National Health System — there were only a few beds and a small nursing staff, but everyone felt at least a stand against bureaucracy had been made — and she had begged to be allowed to stay there, among the people she knew, instead of being sent to the faceless city hospital . . . she kept repeating to everyone that she felt perfectly well, it had been some kind of temporary thing, all she was thankful for was that she hadn't been holding young Tom at the time.

There had been X-rays and tests,

Doctor Clarke had called in a specialist from London, at first it had seemed like a stroke, but after endless discussions and questions, this idea had been proved wrong.

'You just lie there and learn to have some patience, my girl,' Doctor Clarke had smiled down at her, 'the rest will do you good, you drive yourself too hard, and I've told matron to feed you up, you're far too thin.'

Kate didn't tell him she'd been on a strict self-inflicted diet since her marriage, terrified of putting on extra weight and losing her figure, neither did she say that trying to keep up with a husband ten years younger than yourself, was no easy task — in any case it didn't matter now — Larry had gone, she'd driven him away with her stupid suspicion, and the whole purpose and meaning of her life had gone with him . . . what matter if she did get fat, wrinkled, grey now, there was no one to notice, no one to care.

She'd had to tell Roz about the row

she and Larry had had. 'It was all my fault, I accused him of all sorts of things I know in my heart weren't true, I don't know what got into me, I suppose it's this wretched complex I have about our ages. I know you think it doesn't matter, but it does, his having left me proves it.' She buried her face in the pillow as the tears poured down her cheeks.

Roz was at her wits' end to know what to do — both Dr Clarke and the matron had asked where Larry was — he should be at her side, that was what she needed more than anything.

At first, to protect what was left of Kate's pride, she had told them he had had to go away to do a commission of some kind — she wasn't sure where, but as their insistence that he must be sent for grew, she had to tell them she had no idea where he was.

'Could he have gone to relations? To friends perhaps,' the doctor asked.

Roz shook her head, 'I don't think he has any relations, Mum told me he was brought up in an Orphanage, and I don't even know where he came from to Kingsford Grammar School.'

They were sitting in the surgery after hours where Roz had gone to talk to him, he poured her a glass of sherry.

'I'm not going to beat about the bush, I've known you and your mother for too long to try and pull any wool over your eyes,' he paused a moment, 'what you choose to tell her is your own affair.'

Roz felt the colour drain from her face, 'You mean she's never going to get better?'

He shook his head, 'With these kind of diseases of the nervous system, possibly degenerative, we can't tell, we shall have to do more tests as time passes. She's very anaemic, and this is associated with the disease, but in all cases of this kind it is the patient who can often do more than the doctor.'

Roz hesitated for a moment, 'Then I think, knowing Mum, there's only one thing to do, to tell her the truth.'

He nodded, 'I agree entirely.'

And so it was arranged that Roz should be there when he visited Kate the next morning . . . meanwhile she spent a sleepless night, tossing and turning — if only she could find Larry, bring him back, somehow she had the feeling his very presence would help to cure her mother . . . but where to start looking? Maybe she ought to go to the police, or tell the newspapers, but she knew he'd hate that kind of publicity, and so would Kate when she found out.

She dragged herself from bed the next morning, bathed and fed young Tom, took Fred for a walk, but even the mild beauty of the day couldn't penetrate her mood of depression. How to face Kate with the possibility of no real cure — Kate who had always been so energetic, so involved in life.

As she reached the gate to the garden she saw there was a car standing in the drive. Oh dear, she thought, the last thing I can face at the moment is a visitor . . . maybe it's someone wanting

Larry to do a painting . . . what on earth can I tell them?

But as she rounded the corner of the lawn she felt a moment of relief and joy, for coming towards her was no one else but Larry himself. He looked haggard and pale, his hair dishevelled, a growth of beard on his face. 'Hullo Roz, I came for some paints and stuff, couldn't make anyone hear though. I thought Kate must be in, her car's in the garage.'

Fred had thrown himself against Larry in an ecstasy of welcome, he was missing Kate and his beloved master, in fact the whole small world had gone topsy turvy in the last few days, he'd never spent so much time shut in the kitchen.

For a moment it seemed odd that Larry didn't know about Kate, it was over a fortnight since she'd been taken ill, but to Roz it felt like a lifetime — now she had to tell him, and there was no point in trying to soften the blow . . . in any case she didn't know what his true feelings were, she'd only heard Kate's side of the quarrel. But for all she knew he might have been with Stephanie — she'd heard the girl had gone to London to work for some charitable organization. Anyhow where men were concerned, judging by her own experience, you couldn't tell.

He stood looking at her, waiting for her answer, and by the expression on Roz's face he had guessed something was wrong. He grabbed her arm — 'Roz, has something happened? To Kate . . . has she gone away — had an accident?'

Roz shook her head, 'Not exactly, but she's ill Larry, she was taken ill,' she hesitated a moment, 'the night you went away, I had to get the doctor and an ambulance, get her into hospital.'

'She didn't,' he broke in, then stopped, not able to bring himself to utter the words.

Roz gave a ghost of a smile, 'No, she didn't do anything silly, it's some kind of nervous complaint, she's at Kingsford, I don't think it's exactly serious, and yet in a way it is. It's difficult to explain, the best thing would be to come along this morning with me to the hospital, Doctor Clarke's going to be there — I'll have a word with him, see if it's O.K.'

Larry had gone so white that for a moment Roz thought he might faint. 'My God, you don't mean it's something I did, or said?'

Roz shook her head, touching his arm lightly as if he were a child who must be reassured, 'No, it's just one of those things that would have happened anyway, even the specialist isn't sure of the cause . . . look, come inside and I'll make a cup of coffee, and ring the doctor.'

He followed her with bowed shoulders. Suddenly he looked an old man.

9

Kate lay with her eyes half closed — the hospital day ebbed and flowed without touching her, except in the routine of washing, eating, medicines and so on . . . when the door opened she didn't take much notice, it would be the nurse, or the doctor, or Roz . . . all kind and helpful, but not the face she wanted to see.

Now she felt rather than saw, someone standing by the bed, there was a faint smell of tobacco — and something else she couldn't place for a moment — paint — that was it, and turps . . . her eyes flew open. Wearily she passed the back of one hand across her eyes, she must be dreaming, it looked like Larry, only an older Larry, with lines on his face she didn't remember . . . and a beard . . . she felt warm lips on her cheek, and her name murmured . . . 'Kate, my poor darling, precious Kate . . . ' Then his arms were round her, drawing her to him as she felt the rough tweed of his jacket, the prickle of his unshaven face.

'Larry . . . oh Larry . . . I've longed for you, wanted you so much, don't ever leave me again my darling.'

He perched on the edge of the bed, caressing her, murmuring to her tenderly as if she were a small child, until at last she smiled.

'If only I'd known, if only my stupid pride hadn't stopped me phoning,' he said it over and over again.

'Never mind, you're here now, I must get better, come home to look after you.' She tried to push herself up in the bed. 'It's so silly, I feel perfectly O.K. in myself, but first I couldn't move my arms, they're better now, but my legs . . . '

Before she could say any more the doctor and Roz came into the room, smiling at Kate and Larry.

'That's better, a happy patient is

halfway to being a cured patient,' the doctor rubbed his hands, 'Now Kate, having had a chat with both Roz and Larry, I've come to the conclusion it's best to explain your condition to you — as far as I can, mainly because I think you're the sensible kind of person who can help yourself.'

'I agree,' Larry said quickly, 'and if she can come home, I'll nurse her myself.'

'We'll see, all in good time, she needs to stay here for a little while though . . . you see this is a kind of muscular atrophy, which I expect you've all heard of, but it is in fact a whole group of diseases, in most of them some kind of damage occurs to the nervous system.'

'Do you mean permanently?' Kate's voice was very low.

'Not necessarily. The specialist assures me it can be treated in fact. It is what is called subacute degeneration that gave you the feeling of numbness — of paralysis. It isn't easy at this moment to tell how much damage has been done, usually it's the sheaths which are wrapped round the nerve fibres which suffer. A lot of work is being done on this subject, both here and in America.'

Kate had stopped listening — she said quickly, 'Do you mean I am going to be an invalid, partly paralysed for the rest of my life? I'd rather know.'

Larry picked up her hand, holding it close . . .

The doctor smiled reassuringly at them. 'Gracious no. This is a kind of random loss of sensation, or movement, the trouble is there are no two cases alike, which makes it difficult to diagnose. And it can smoulder like a damped down bonfire so no one can really tell how quickly or slowly it will progress — it might be years, or never, before there is another attack. Neurology is full of mystery diseases.'

'I'd like to know exactly what all this means as far as I'm concerned,' Kate said, her eyes on his face.

'My dear Kate, I wish I could tell you. All I can say is that the symptoms you have may vanish altogether, already as you know the paralysis has gone from your arms and hands — although it has attacked your legs, but I'm sure only temporarily. We can help in various ways and I can't see any reason why you shouldn't return to perfect health — it's just that I'm not going to guarantee a complete cure, as if you were suffering from measles or jaundice.'

Seeing the anguish on Larry's face, the doctor put his hand on his shoulder, 'Look — don't worry, Kate's got a marvellous constitution, and a normally cheerful disposition, with your help personally I think it's only a matter of weeks before she really will be back to normal.'

And so the uphill task of rehabilitation began. Gradually the feeling started to return to her legs, and Doctor Clarke insisted she try to use them, 'Much of the recovery is in your own hands, and controlled exercise is one of the chief cures.'

'It's all very well for you to say that,' Kate smiled ruefully, 'but my wretched muscles won't listen to you — or me. They seem like blocks of wood.' But in a kind of desperation now, she knew she had to get better for Larry's sake. He'd given up everything, his painting, all his other interests, to devote every minute to her.

The physiotherapist bullied her unceasingly into more and more effort — 'Work hard, Mrs Stafford,' she barked at Kate as she straddled the exercise bicycle, 'try to really press down hard on the pedals.'

Some nights, as she lay alone in the narrow hospital bed, she cried herself to sleep — sometimes near hopelessness and utter weariness filled her — sometimes defeat seemed inevitable. She knew her illness and incapacity must be a trial to Larry, a burden, but he spent all day with her, talking, reading, sometimes just sitting and holding her hand. Never had he been so gentle, so thoughtful of the terrible night of their quarrel, and where he had been for those two long weeks, while she lay ill, they never spoke. Maybe one day he would tell her, but she felt she really had no right to spy.

Sometimes she did long to say, 'Darling, you're young, you've no business to be tied to a middle aged invalid, I'm useless to you like this,' wanting to be reassured . . . and as if he guessed, he'd bend down and kiss her.

'Kate, I love you, does it matter how long it takes? We've got forever, and between us we're going to get you well.'

'Oh my love,' she said softly, 'I'm the one who has to get well, to fight — you have your own life to live.'

'Yes,' he replied gently, 'it is my life, and I'll live it with you, no matter what happens. I know without you I have no life.'

And then, just as suddenly as the paralysis had struck, it vanished. One day Kate sat on the edge of the bed, Larry took her hands in his and she stood up . . . for a moment she thought she would fall back, the muscles were weak and the flesh had gone, leaving them like two sticks, but he drew her to her feet.

'You can do it, love, you wiggled your toes and pressed against the bottom of the bed, the feeling's coming back, it's only a matter of trying to walk now.'

She stood clinging to his hands, trembling with sudden nervousness, her eyes wide with fear and anticipation. He took a little step backwards, encouraging her to follow, she could feel sweat on her face and hands, but slowly the muscles responded to her will, she slid her right foot forwards, again he took a small step backwards, and then caught her in his arms as tears of happiness and exhaustion ran down her cheeks.

He held her close for a moment, feeling the return of the old passion and warmth; for the first time in weeks she laughed spontaneously as he whispered, 'You're all right sweetheart, soon you'll be able to do everything you want, be back to my darling, normal Kate.'

She nodded, too full of emotion to speak. He picked her up in his arms, feeling how light she had become, the bones stuck through the flesh, she buried her face in his shoulder.

'Oh Larry, how could I live without you? If it hadn't been for you I'd just have given up.'

'No, not you Kate, but all people need people.'

'And specially I need you,' she whispered against the softness of his hair as he laid her slender body tenderly on the bed and kissed her passionately on the lips.

Soon Kate was well enough to go home, having given Doctor Clarke her solemn word to take life more easily. 'Although I don't mean from the exercise point of view,' he grinned, 'you must walk all you can so long as you don't tire yourself.'

'Silly old fusspot he is,' she said to Larry as they sat either side of the fire back at the mill, while Roz was upstairs putting young Tom to bed, 'I've never felt fitter in my life than I do now, how about fixing up a skiing holiday — that ought to strengthen my leg muscles?'

Larry threw back his head and laughed, 'Kate you're incorrigible, we'll go to Switzerland or Austria — wherever you want, but quite honestly I don't think he meant you to be as active as that!'

Fred came padding into the room, wagging his tail, overjoyed to have his beloved mistress back at home, thrusting his cold, wet nose into her hand. 'There you are,' Larry said, 'that's the best way to start, as Fred suggests, a gentle walk or two.' He got up and went over to where she sat, stroking the dog's silky head and ears. He kissed her gently on the lips, and she felt the passion and fire he always arose in her, run swiftly along her nerves . . . she lifted her fingers to her mouth where he had touched it — at that moment Roz came into the room and thought what a delightful group they made . . . while Kate thought how beautiful she looked in the long kaftan, scarlet as holly berries, a matching ribbon tying back her hair, and she wished with all her heart she could conjure up just the right man for her . . . she gave a little sigh.

Roz bent and kissed her. 'Mum, you're tired, I shall send you right off to bed, it's my turn to be boss now, with the help of my step-daddy of course!' Her eyes twinkled as she went over and put her arm lightly on Larry's shoulders, laughing up at him.

'Funny thing is,' she went on, 'since Mum's been in hospital the difference between you two seems to have narrowed, as far as years are concerned I mean — she looks much better for the rest,' she paused a moment. 'I suppose it's not a very tactful thing to say, but perhaps it doesn't matter so much with a man — you do look more — well perhaps mature is the word,' she giggled at Larry.

He laughed, 'Why don't you just say older, daughter, and be damned!' He poured a glass of sherry for them all. ‘Let’s drink to the future — the future of all of us, and that of course includes that lusty young man upstairs — it’s nice to be a complete family again.’ He went and sat on the arm of Kate’s chair as she smiled up at him. And how dear that family is, she thought — but how small and vulnerable my world.

10

On Christmas Eve they all went to the midnight service — Jessie came from the village to babysit with young Tom. Larry had bought Kate a coloured television for Christmas, secretly proud that now he had money of his own to buy her presents. Jessie almost fell over herself with anxiety to be allowed to watch — baby sitting would be no hardship with the telly for company.

The ancient village church was warm and cosy, both with the heat from the old-fashioned coke stove, and the crowd of people who filled the pews. At first Kate thought some of them might be a bit offhandish, she hadn't seen much of them since her marriage, but many had been kind while she was in hospital, and brought flowers and fruit when they heard of her illness — now they seemed pleased she had made such a good recovery.

There was something about the Christmas service that always brought a lump to Kate's throat — the old familiar carols, the sight of the fresh-faced choir boys in their scarlet and white with starched frills under their chins . . . they looked like small angels, but she knew better, ten to one they had a catapult hidden under the pew, or were planning some other devilment, like most healthy boys of their age.

The decorations of holly and evergreens were bright to see, and the perfume of fir and spruce that hung on the air, filled Kate with bitter sweet nostalgia — so many times she and Tom had been to this little church — when they married, when Roz had been christened, for Easter and at Christmas . . . she could almost imagine he stood beside her now, and it was comforting to feel as if his spirit still lingered.

She came back to the present with a jolt — Roz and Larry were singing at the top of their voices — both of them way off key, but, she thought with a smile, their obvious enjoyment made up for lack of performance. At that moment Larry turned and gave her an enormous wink as if he had guessed what she was thinking . . . then the vicar was reading the epistle for Christmas Day, and she found a strange comfort in the closing words . . . 'They all shall wax old as doth a garment; and as a vesture shalt thou fold them up, and they shall be changed; but thou art the same, and thy years shall not fail . . .'

Although it was very quiet, with just the four of them, it was one of the best Christmas times Kate could remember — Boxing Day brought a flurry of snow and they spent the time indoors, reading, talking, playing backgammon and listening to music — 'and I've eaten far too much!' Kate laughed, so even when the next day it started to rain, she decided it was time both she and Fred had some exercise.

Now he was assured of Kate's return to health, Larry had started work on some of the commissions he had shelved when she was ill.

The dog was in the kitchen, sitting with drooling jaws waiting for Jessie to throw him some scraps from the cold turkey. 'Honestly I think he'd eat till he burst!' Kate said, drawing on her old duffle coat and opening the glass door that led into the garden.

She stood for a moment looking up through the bare branches of the apple trees, as she gazed at the heavy leaden sky she felt a little stab of unhappiness — December was a sad month, water dripped on to the sodden grass, the leat ran full and noisily past the silent mill wheel, and a flock of crows rose squawking and quarrelling from the ploughed field beyond the orchard. The words of a favourite poem came unbidden into her mind — 'They are not long, the weeping and the laughter, Love and desire and hate . . . They are not long, the days of wine and roses.'

Ernest Dowson had written those words nearly a hundred years ago. She wondered if they had meant anything to him personally . . . suddenly she realized she had been standing gazing at the mill wheel, exactly on the spot where Larry had stood that first summer when they had met, when he had come to do the painting which had seen the dawn of their love. In such a short time they had come a long way, experienced much, now, on the verge of a new year, she prayed the future might be peaceful, that she might hold his love . . . and as she stood with the pale December sun catching the lights in her hair, a few tears ran slowly down her cheeks — maybe they had been some kind of presentiment, for on New Year's Day the dreaded pins and needles started once more in her fingers and hands . . . Larry made her stay in bed while he sent for Doctor Clarke.

He looked grave as he examined her, but he said, 'I think we may have caught it in time, keeping you resting from the onset of the feeling.'

But Kate wouldn't be comforted, nothing either he or Larry or Roz said would pacify her, she lay with her face turned to the wall, desolate, drained of all emotion, except for a great wave of self-pity and sorrow, partly for herself, and partly for Larry that he had to suffer all this again.

However to her delight and surprise, when she woke from the sedative the doctor had given her, no paralysis had attacked her this time, and after a week resting in bed, even the pins and needles had disappeared. She got up, pale and shaky, but at least mobile . . . she could scarcely believe her good luck.

Doctor Clarke smiled, 'I did tell you it might happen, that we know so little about these nervous diseases,' he paused, 'however I have been wondering . . . I'd like Larry to be here to listen to what I have to suggest, Kate.'

She glanced at him apprehensively.

'It's all right,' he reassured her,

'nothing terrible — just that a new Clinic has been opened in America, just outside, or in the suburbs of Washington. A Doctor Luftsen has done a great deal of research and experimenting with nervous troubles. He has had some amazing successes, particularly with your type of attack.'

'You mean he might be able totally to cure me — so I never have another attack?' Kate asked.

The doctor shook his head, 'I'm not being trapped into passing out guarantees,' he smiled, 'no one can be sure, but at least after tests and so on, he will be able to tell you if there is a chance, and then if you wish, you can stay and have treatment, usually it's about a month attending his clinic, then you will be able to finish it at home here.'

Larry put his arm round Kate, 'It sounds like a fairy tale. Has he a good record of success?'

The doctor nodded, 'Yes, as high as 70% — but of course all the symptoms vary, I don't know how many cases identical with Kate's he's had through his hands.' He paused, 'Of course it isn't everyone who can afford it either, I'm afraid it doesn't come under the National Health!'

Larry thrust his hands into the pockets of his jeans, 'That's no problem now thank heavens, 'I've got a nice little nest egg, if it costs every penny we've got, to have Kate restored to complete health is all that matters.'

And so they made the necessary arrangements. It took many transatlantic telephone calls, cables, and so on, for the Clinic only had limited space, and these had to be serious cases. Dr Luftsen's secretary had to have all the details of Kate's illness before she could be admitted, and then some kind of outside accommodation had to be found near the Clinic.

At first this seemed rather difficult from so far away, but as luck would have it, when Roz had been in America and visited Washington, among the people she'd met were a couple who were shortly coming to England for a holiday — maybe they might want to rent their house — it was a chance worth exploring anyway. She rang them, explaining the position and they said they would be delighted to let Kate and Larry have the house for as long as they needed it, as they were in England, they could let them have the keys before they left . . . it did seem as if luck was on their side, and on a bitterly cold February day Roz drove them to the airport, clinging to her mother as they parted and for a moment, as Kate looked at young Tom, and a rather forlorn Roz, she was almost tempted not to leave . . . but Larry stood a little impatiently, and she knew there was no going back now on her decision.

It was dusk when eventually they reached Washington. The taxi drove them down a broad avenue that shone with coloured electric signs and the lights of endless streams of cars. At first they thought it must be some kind of gala night, every house seemed to have its porch light turned on, the square glass canopies outside the theatres and picture houses were a dazzle of jewelled lights, but the driver said — 'It's just an ordinary evening I guess — most American cities are like this at night, and after all, how about your own Piccadilly Circus? That was well lit up when I was over visiting last fall.'

'Yes,' Larry said slowly, 'I suppose you're right, we just never noticed.'

The house turned out to be the All-American open plan, split level dream, with every labour-saving device imaginable — a bathroom and shower to each bedroom, T.V. sets everywhere . . . they stood gazing round with some bewilderment, it was so different from the rather old-fashioned but cosy mill, — more like some lush film set.

'I feel almost afraid to sit down,' Larry whispered. At that moment the door chimes sounded.

Two women stood on the step. 'Welcome,' they said as if it were a rehearsed piece, but their smiles were warm. 'We live just across the road, we've brought some Welcome Wagon gifts. There were flowers, a guide to Washington with pictures, signed by some of the other neighbours, 'To the visitors from England — Welcome.'

There were plates of cakes, fruit, pizzas — enough food to last for a month Kate felt . . . they were invited to dinner, to parties, to hunting trips — Larry tried to explain about Kate's illness and the fact they would be leading a very quiet life, but of course anyone would be welcome to call any time — to visit — he added, seeing their rather puzzled expressions at the word 'call'. They were more interested and sympathetic than ever, saying that Dr Luftsen was becoming a legend, even after the short time he'd been at the Clinic. They left at last, assuring Kate just to let them know if there was anything at all they could do.

Larry had hired a car, but he was glad it was only a short way to the Clinic for the different system of traffic control, and the enormous car with its automatic box, confused him at first, but fortunately as they were in the suburbs the road wasn't too crowded. As they drove they were fascinated by the charming houses, and there were trees everywhere, in the gardens and the streets, trees and broad avenues — Roz had told them Washington was reputed to be the most beautiful city in America, and even Kate, who didn't like towns, couldn't believe that any city could have been made so delightful.

The clinic too was a kind of dream. It consisted of two houses in a large garden, which had been joined by a glass corridor. It stood in a quiet district not far from Dumbarton Oaks Park, and they were surprised how peaceful and almost countrified it was. The Director of Nurses met them in the entrance hall. A rather formidable looking lady, who told them her name was Mrs Nicholson, however under the starchy bosom they soon found a heart of gold.

'We have more staff than patients,' she smiled at them, 'our main concern is for your care and comfort, Mrs Stafford. Doctor is very keen on the positive approach.'

Kate began to feel nervous at the thought of meeting the great man as they followed the nurse along thickly carpeted corridors from whose windows they could see great clumps of purple and gold crocuses, making Kate exclaim, 'It looks just like England!'

Mrs Nicholson smiled, 'The gardens were laid out by an Englishman, I think he must have been homesick for it is full of English flowers and plants.' She knocked on a door simply marked 'Director'. A deep voice called, 'Come!'

Dr Luftsen was sitting at a huge desk, dressed all in white and smiling at them. He got to his feet and held out his hand. He was tall and thin with a balding head surrounded by a little frill of hair. He had a long thin neck, with an over active Adam's apple, and he reminded Kate of a long legged bird so that she had an almost overwhelming desire to laugh, which relieved the tension that had built up inside her . . . he had a charming smile and manner and she soon forgot his appearance.

'Tomorrow there will be tests, many tests, until you are fed up,' he grinned, 'then we can start treatment. But this will only take up a small part of your day, and provided you get plenty of rest, you and your husband may spend some of the day exploring our beautiful city — while the weather is kind. It is good for the mind to have a change too.'

He gave Kate a diet sheet. 'This is very important, I want you to keep to it exactly,' — Kate thought briefly of all the food piled up back at the house. — 'and to relax,' the doctor went on. 'This is vital, for often this disease can be caused by stress and worry — you see an upset in blood circulation, breathing, can very easily damage nerve cells,' he paused and grinned, 'Am I being too long winded and boring?'

Kate smiled back and shook her head, 'No, as a matter of fact I feel more reassured every minute, just listening to you!'

In a way it was like a second honeymoon, like the holiday they had promised themselves and never had. The first few days Kate had to spend some hours at the Clinic, being examined, tests of sensation and muscular movements, even taste, smell, vision and speech came under scrutiny, and both she and Larry waited with some trepidation for all the information to be collated.

On the third morning the doctor smiled broadly at Kate. 'Well, if it hadn't been for your doctor's detailed report, I would say you were a fraud!' he paused and burst out laughing at Kate's expression. 'I can find nothing organically wrong, and there has already been some healing of the damaged nerves, but you are anaemic, you need feeding up on the right food, and natural remedies — apart from injections and some electric wave therapy, also a daily swim in the heated pool.'

'And that's all?' Kate could hardly believe her ears.

He nodded. 'When you leave this Clinic, provided you are careful not to get over-tired, to eat properly, there is no reason why you should have another attack of the paralysis.' He hesitated a moment, 'There is only one thing Mrs Stafford, and this I have to tell you. I don't know if you and your husband already have a family, or if you plan to have any more . . . ' Kate glanced at him swiftly.

'Why do you ask that?'

For a moment he dropped his eyes, carefully balancing a paper knife on his fingers. 'Because sometimes the injections, and other forms of treatment we give, can make a woman barren.'

For a moment all the joy over his former words drained away from Kate. In her heart she had never given up hoping that she would have Larry's child, had even hoped that the treatment for her illness might help in some way . . . but now this was a body blow she'd never anticipated.

She raised her eyes to his, 'Suppose — in view of that — I decided not to have the treatment, just to go back home?'

He got up abruptly, 'In that case I couldn't be responsible for the results of course.' He stood with his back to her, looking across the garden, warm and bright in the spring sunshine, in the distance could be heard the laughter and chatter of children, making Kate catch her breath on a half sob . . . he was going on, 'But without meaning to be rude or personal, does it matter much at your age that you cannot have a child?'

He swung round, 'If you don't carry on with the treatment, there is every possibility you may one day be completely paralysed . . . I think you should realize that.'

Quietly, briefly, Kate explained about her marriage, about the difference in her's and Larry's ages, and the fact that he longed for a child.

He gave her a keen look, 'From what I have seen of your husband Mrs Stafford, I would say that your life and health are more important to him than an unborn child . . . given the choice.'

Kate got unsteadily to her feet, resting a hand on the desk for a moment, 'Then I think that I must give him that choice,' she said softly.

Larry had been exploring Washington, but when she got back he could see by her expression that all was not well. He drew her quickly into his arms. 'What is it darling? Is it worse than we thought, tell me.'

She couldn't stop the tears now as he soothed her gently like a child as she clung to him, sobbing.

Tenderly he dried her eyes with his handkerchief as she told him.

'It isn't that — in fact I'm better than we dared hope, I still have to have treatment — diet, injections and so on,' she paused, 'and that's the trouble, it means there's every chance I'll never be able to have a child . . . so it's a choice between the two.' She raised her eyes to his. All she saw there was love and a great tenderness as he bent to kiss her.

'There isn't any question of choice darling Kate. To get you well is all that matters.'

In the days that followed their love seemed to have developed a new sympathy, a depth of understanding that hadn't been there before. They would lie in bed at night, talking, going back over the years before they'd met. Once he'd said, 'I suppose in a way I never really knew what love was as a child — caring and interest yes, but not love, not total involvement, belonging.'

'And perhaps because of your artistic nature, that hurt more even than it might have a less sensitive child,' she said gently.

He drew her into his arms. 'Maybe. But life has a way of compensating, of evening out the score, for since I met you I have all the love I need, child or no child . . . maybe we could adopt one when we get back to England . . . perhaps even Roz would let us have Tom!'

'I don't know about that,' Kate said slowly. 'He means a great deal to her, a kind of compensation for Dick . . . still, perhaps if she should fall in love and want to get married.' She snuggled down in his arms, 'Let's not worry, let's just see what happens.' She kissed his shoulder and once more the wonder and passion of their love swept through her and she felt more fulfilled, more satisfied than she ever had.

They were like children released from school — the spring weather was warm and sunny, they went to Art Galleries, the Smithsonian Institute, the Department of Justice and toured the F.B.I. Headquarters, they visited the White House, surprised at its hotch potch of architecture, but finding the rambling white building all windows and porticoes, charming as it stood in its own green park in the very heart of the city.

'Washington might have been built for lovers,' Larry said as one evening they drove back from Virginia where they had spent the day. Darkness fell, there was a moment when the sky was pale turquoise touched with gold, and the bare trees stood against it like lace, each twig defined and crisp, the buildings like a collage of glowing squares on a black background. The street lamps were lit, but gave no light as yet, it was dark, and yet it wasn't, as the sky faded to amethyst and the day was over. But the night hadn't really begun . . . a timeless moment, detached and caught briefly in suspense, so clearly etched in Kate's mind . . . they crossed the Arlington Memorial Bridge and the full moon rose turning the Lindon Memorial all ghostly glowing in white marble in the park along the river's edge. The city seemed to be made up of mock classic buildings, and they gazed at the beauty and she could tell Larry was absorbing it all into his artist's mind to reproduce later on canvas. His hand sought and held hers in a warm grasp, and for a moment she knew such an intense happiness it was almost too much to bear.

11

Kate hadn't really enjoyed the jet flight to America, secretly she was scared of planes and flying, so they decided, as there was no desperate hurry, to go home by boat. Larry managed to get a couple of cancellations on a Greek boat which was making an eight day transatlantic crossing as it returned to England to pick up passengers for a cruise to the Caribbean.

'A sea change — it'll just put the finishing touches to the cure.' Dr Luftsen was delighted, as he was in the whole progress that Kate had made. As they said their good-byes, they thanked him and left with regret for he had become more of a friend than a doctor and he promised if he ever came to England, he would visit them.

Kate's only experience of a boat before had been on a channel steamer

— huddled under a coat on a windy deck because people were being sick below, so this lazy, luxurious life, was a completely new concept as far as ships were concerned.

The prospect of meeting people, making friends and then probably never seeing them again was intriguing as you floated in a complete, detached world.

On the second day out from New York she sat in a deck chair, trying to read, but more often lifting her eyes to the sun specked sea that dipped beyond the rail, and to the procession of walkers who paced their mile round the deck.

Larry was having a game of quoits with the two small children of the American couple who had the next cabin to theirs and shared their table at meals.

Early on in their exchanges of backgrounds and home life, they had discovered they'd seen Roz riding in the show when she was in America. They couldn't get over what a small world it was, meeting her 'mom' like this, and Kate was secretly amused at the fascination she and Larry seemed to have for them because America was a woman's world, where the husband still looked after the wife, and was nearly always the elder of the two — they were intrigued that Larry should be ten years younger than Kate, and yet so attentive.

The voices of the players came to her softly on the salty breeze — they sounded so young — the word which had assumed such importance in her life — sometimes even now, in spite of all his reassurance, and the fact that he'd nursed her through illness and convalescence, she still felt vulnerable, like a crab without its shell, when people realized the age gap. Even if they didn't refer to it. She was still conscious of it. Once someone had told her that during middle age the young simply seem to be getting younger. 'Then there suddenly comes a day when you look at them, and see that really they're at least in their 30s — and still much younger than you. And then you realize what that makes you!'

But she was glad of the Allans' company — they were both about Larry's age, the wife a little woman with a monkey kind of face, but her husband, Rod, adored her. After they'd been introduced she went on smiling, and said, 'Please call me Sharon, everyone does.'

They had two small boys of 10 and 8 — inclined to be prococious, like most American children, but they still had nice manners, and although it was obvious their parents idolized them, they were strict. The family was on its way to visit Ireland where their ancestors had come from, although they were also very proud that they lived in Boston — 'In a way we feel near home,' Rod had said, 'You see after all Boston is the heart of New England.'

Kate and Larry rose late, having their breakfast brought to the cabin, and now she longed to be home again, to see Roz and young Tom, and Fred . . . and the garden at the mill in all the glory of spring, she'd never been away from home so long before. They talked of some alterations they would make, of how young Tom would have changed, even if Fred would have forgotten them.

'And I can hardly wait to get back to work now,' Larry smiled at her. 'I've been very lazy for too long.' He flexed his fingers, 'Almost forgotten what it feels like to hold a brush — and just think of all the commissions piling up — I hope!'

Kate laughed, 'You know even if they're not, you've got enough work to keep you going for years.' Suddenly she was serious, 'Larry we're so lucky, we seem to have everything,' she paused, 'Well, almost everything.'

He took her hand and gently kissed the palm. 'Let's hope the Gods didn't hear you say that, they have a nasty habit of slapping you down if they think things are going too well!'

She felt a sudden shiver of coldness at his words . . . then he said, 'Come on, race you to the deck, I promised to teach the boys the rules of English cricket, and you and Sharon can have some of what she calls 'Girls' talk' about the latest fashions. I can't really think why they gave the poor girl such a name, anything less like 'Sharon's dewy rose' I can't imagine.'

There was a fancy dress dance that night, Kate had been whirled round the room by both Larry and Rod, she felt quite young and carefree once more, and then she sat watching Larry, who seemed to be everywhere at once, and the applause was deafening when he and Sharon won the spot prize — a table lighter which he insisted she should keep as he didn't smoke — 'At least only a pipe,' he laughed, 'and a lighter's useless for that.'

'He does keep the match industry going,' Kate said, joining in the fun for everyone had gathered round the winning couple. It had been a very popular result for everyone seemed to like Larry.

All too quickly the voyage was nearly over, the last night they sat up late, talking, laughing, promising to meet again, to write, exchanging addresses. 'I'll go and get my address book, I left it in the cabin,' Kate said, but Larry jumped to his feet and pushed her gently back into her chair.

'You just sit there and finish your drink, I'll get it.'

Sharon watched him walk away and sighed, 'He's dishy, honey. You're so lucky, both of you — not that I'd change my Rod for anyone, but he's not exactly Paul Newman,' she giggled, 'Still no one could call me Liz Taylor either.'

Kate smiled and drained her glass. Suddenly there was some kind of commotion at the other end of the room and the Chief Officer came quickly towards them, his face white with anxiety.

'Mrs Allan — Mrs Stafford, could

you come with me, there's been a slight accident.'

The colour drained from the women's faces as their thoughts flew to husband, children.

'Please don't worry too much, I'm sure everything will be all right,' his voice was not very convincing.

By this time a little crowd had gathered and Rod had come across from the bar. 'What is it? What's happened?' Without replying the officer shepherded them across the floor and out of the door before anyone could ask any more questions. He opened the lift doors and bundled them in. 'Please, what is it?' Kate insisted, trying to stop her knees from trembling.

'There was a small fire in Mr and Mrs Allan's cabin — fortunately Mr Stafford smelt the smoke and arrived in time to save either of the boys from being badly burnt, the blankets were smouldering — but I don't really know any details, it seems they were playing with a cigarette lighter.'

'But Larry — Mr Stafford — is he hurt?' Kate's voice broke. The officer put his hand on her shoulder, 'Nothing serious I'm sure, the doctor is with him now, it was just his hands, they got burnt when he put out the flames — but I'm sure you needn't worry, Mrs Stafford, he's not unsconscious or anything like that.'

'Only his hands!' Kate thought, 'Please God don't let it be bad.' She buried her face in Rod's shoulder as he put his arm round her.

'Don't worry honey, I'm sure everything'll be O.K.'

The cabin wasn't very big and it seemed to be crammed with people, there was the acrid smell of burnt wool hanging on the air, and the chemical from the extinguisher formed a big patch on the carpet. The two boys stood either side of the stewardess, who had her arms round them, their eyes big with fear; Larry sat slumped in a small armchair, his face ashen, his eyes closed, as the doctor bent over him, cutting away the scorched sleeves of his shirt and coat. Kate flew to him and knelt down, oblivious of the other people, as he opened his eyes and looked at her.

'Kate, it's my hands. I can't feel anything in them at all, tell me they're not badly burnt.'

She glanced swiftly at the doctor, he shook his head gently . . . she could see the scorched flesh and what looked like a piece of bone protruding from the tattered skin of the knuckles . . . suddenly everything started to swim around her, she felt as if she were falling into a huge black pit, and above her Larry's face whirled round and round as he called her name . . . gradually getting further and further away until at last she couldn't hear him, she was totally alone.

Everyone was very kind. The Allans simply couldn't do enough for Kate, treating her like a child, but nothing could take away the knowledge that Larry's hands were so severely burned that it was impossible for the ship's doctor to tell her what the outcome would be.

A helicopter had flown him to Southampton, for although they were within sight of land, swiftness of treatment was essential, and the doctor said the delay in waiting for the boat to dock might make a difference between saving his hands even.

He gave Kate a sedative, and made her stay in her cabin. Unfortunately there hadn't been room for her to go in the helicopter, but the Allans had promised to see all the luggage through customs, and she was given immediate clearance directly the boat docked.

'He saved their lives — my babies,' Sharon said over and over again. 'There's nothing too much we can do honey. If only he wasn't an artist, so that his hands matter so much.'

Although Kate was grateful for their kindness and help, for she felt numb, incapable of dealing with anything herself, there were times when she wanted only to be alone, if she couldn't be with Larry and share his agony . . . she felt exhausted, useless, and although she'd managed to talk to the hospital by radio telephone, since Larry had arrived there, they didn't tell her much. He had been flown on to London and was getting the best attention, was as comfortable as could be expected — the trite, impersonal phrases.

She had lain down, suddenly completely deflated, there were only a few hours before the boat docked, a few hours before she saw Larry, the Allans had made all the arrangements, from that point of view she had nothing to think about, they just couldn't show their gratitude enough — but what was Larry going to do if he could never paint again? Never hold a brush . . . the words kept going through her head.

She hadn't meant to sleep, but when she opened her eyes it was morning and the sun streamed through the porthole, there was the sound of ceaseless activity on the docks, the shouting of men's voices, ship's sirens, engines, and the cry of gulls. She got up and splashed cold water on her face, and brushed her hair . . . only a few hours now till she saw Larry . . . she half longed, half dreaded the thought.

She didn't remember much about getting off the boat, or the journey . . . she just left everything to the Allans.

When she got to the hospital she was shown to the side ward where he lay. He turned a white, drawn face that she would have hardly recognized — he looked like an old man.

Neither of them spoke as she knelt by the bed, her cheek against his, her eyes irresistibly drawn to the two huge bandaged arms that lay immobile on the coverlet, the hands that had created so much beauty — and which might never do so again.

At last he said, through dry, cracked lips, his voice harsh, 'Have you seen the specialist?'

Kate nodded. She couldn't trust herself to speak.

'I suppose in a way I'm lucky to be alive, and thank God the kids weren't hurt — but it isn't easy Kate.'

'I know love.' Gently she kissed his cheek. 'I know so well. But we'll make out like we did before, only this time I'm the one who has to be strong — things'll work out, you'll see.' The effort to keep the tears from her voice was almost too much.

'We mustn't count on it,' his voice was blurred with drugs and exhaustion.

'Don't talk my love, or they'll send me away. Sister said I was to keep you quiet. Just lie still. At least we're together now, and I'll stay just as long as they'll let me.'

He had closed his eyes, his lashes curved on the pale cheek, his skin looked almost transparent.

'Dear God, let him be all right,' she prayed silently.

A little later he opened his eyes and looked at her. 'Don't leave me, don't ever leave me Kate.' He sounded like a small child, pleading. Her heart yearned with love and pity as she sat on beside him, not saying anything, just watching him, until at last he slept.

After that her days took on a kind of pattern that revolved around the hospital. Roz brought young Tom up to see her for a couple of days at the small hotel where she'd found a room. The baby seemed to have grown and filled out, and Roz looked well although she was desperately worried about Larry — and Kate.

Gradually the days passed, he seemed to get a little more resigned. The specialist had a long talk with Kate. By degrees they were grafting skin to the fingers as they repaired the bones . . . but it was really a question of the muscles and nerves. 'He'll be able to use his hands to a certain extent, Mrs Stafford, I'm pretty certain of that, as far as dressing himself, eating, and so on, but the use and activity is bound to be limited.'

'What about his painting, it's his life,' Kate said slowly.

He shrugged his shoulders, 'That is something we can't forecast.'

She sighed. It seemed to her she had heard those words before — for herself, now they were applied to Larry. She had proved they could be wrong, the doctors — as far as physical health was concerned. 'Is there anything more that can be done, anything at all?' There was a kind of desperation in her voice.

He shook his head, 'No, the bandages come off tomorrow, then it is a case of rehabilitation. He has one thing on his side — youth. That helps of course.'

A month later Larry was discharged from hospital. He still had to have treatment, but this could be done at his local out patients' department.

Roz had lighted the log fire, it was burning brightly when they arrived. She had cooked a meal and filled the house with flowers, for although it was May, the weather was cold and grey.

He sat down in his chair while Roz

poured a drink, and Fred came and laid his head on his knee, gazing up at him adoringly, for in spite of the fact that it was nearly three months since he'd seen his master, the dog hadn't forgotten.

Kate sat on a low stool by his side. 'It's lovely to be home, nothing will ever persuade me to go away again,' she smiled at Roz.

But as the days passed it wasn't easy to keep on assuring him that everything was going to be all right . . . sometimes things went smoothly enough, when Larry seemed almost his old self as they pottered about the garden, and house. As the specialist had foretold, some of the use was returning to his hands, although they were still stiff, and he got frustrated and desperately impatient when he couldn't tie a shoe lace, or do up a button. He couldn't use a knife and fork and Kate had to cut up his food for him . . . as for holding a pencil or brush, that was out of the question. His poor hands were swollen and distorted, so that sometimes Kate couldn't bear even to look at them or touch them. He'd get moody and depressed, and would just sit staring into space. Then Kate couldn't get a word out of him, the misery and resentment showing in his eyes.

She tried to ignore these times, to remind herself that he'd saved the lives of two young children — the Allans had been to see them a couple of times before they returned to Boston — still finding it hard to express their gratitude, and the infinite sadness at the way things had gone for Larry. But bursting with pride, too, unable to contain themselves, that they had traced their ancestors in Ireland and found they were distantly connected to an Irish Count.

Often Kate cried herself to sleep, trying to keep her tears from Larry, but sometimes he would hear her and draw her into his arms, distressed that he was the cause of her grief.

It was a dreary June with long wet periods when the trees dripped damply on the grass and Kate had to force herself to be cheerful, to plan outings for Larry, to interest him in what was going on. The only consolation he seemed to find was in taking Fred for long walks, and playing with young Tom. 'Neither of them notice my hands,' he said bitterly to Kate. Once she found him standing in the studio, staring at the canvasses that lined the walls, trying to pick up the tubes of paint, running his hands down the handles of the brushes and pencils where they stood, gathering dust and cobwebs, in the jars where he had left them.

Quietly she had gone up behind him and put her arms round him, he turned and dropped his head on her breast as sobs were wrenched from his throat in agony . . . and Kate had felt an overwhelming sense of defeat and confusion as she thought of the future.

12

As the days passed it seemed now as though there was a pause in the progress Larry was making. 'I suppose I've reached as far as is possible with the treatment, I might just as well give it up.' His voice was flat, expressionless. 'There isn't much point in keeping on going to the hospital — I'm just where I was weeks ago.'

Kate put her arm round him, 'Don't give up, love. You've done so well, I'm so proud of you.' He'd drawn away, almost roughly, impatient with himself, frustrated and bitter.

'What's the good? I'm useless, a failure,' he dropped his head into his hands.

'I felt that once,' she said quietly, 'when I knew I couldn't have a child, to me that was a failure as a woman, but you convinced me it wasn't so, that your love for me was so great, that it didn't matter. Don't you see? I feel the same about you, we have each other and nothing else matters.'

But he wouldn't be convinced. 'What of the future? How can I go on calling myself a husband if I can't work to keep you? I don't know anything else but painting, and I can't even go back to teaching if I can't show a student how to hold a brush, how to put on colour — 'a useless life is an early death' — Goethe knew how it felt when he said that.'

'Oh Larry,' she said with a touch of impatience. 'What does it matter who has the money? We have enough to live on, in any case it isn't certain that you'll never be able to paint again, it's early days yet, you must have patience.'

But he'd slammed out of the room without answering, and she dropped her head in her hands, feeling utter hopelessness . . . the trouble was she hadn't been feeling too well herself lately and was terrified her own illness might be returning — although the symptoms hadn't been the same — and then — at first she couldn't believe it was possible — she checked and re-checked the dates and, without saying anything to either Roz or Larry, she made an appointment with Doctor Clarke.

She told him of what she suspected, hardly dared to hope . . . he examined her carefully and then grinned at her, almost as excited as she was.

'You're right Kate, I'm certain of it, in about five months . . . it's a wonder no one's noticed you've put on a bit of weight. I can hardly wait to tell Dr Luftsen, he'll be delighted, and surprised. Before the kind of treatment you had has nearly always resulted in a woman becoming barren . . . we must make appointments for you to visit the Ante Natal Clinic regularly, we'll have to keep a special eye on you . . . and I think it would be best if you arrange actually to have the baby in hospital, just to be on the safe side. Perhaps you ought to come in a week before, it's rather difficult in this case to say exactly when it is due.'

Kate hardly took in what he was saying now he had confirmed her hopes. She felt she was walking on air. As she drove home she couldn't make up her mind how to tell Larry . . . his moods nowadays were so uncertain, but he must be as full of joy as she was, this was the fulfilment of all their hopes.

He was out with Fred when she got home. Roz was in the kitchen preparing young Tom's food, and she could tell directly she saw her mother's face that something wonderful had happened.

'Mum, you look as though you've won the pools!'

Kate laughed, 'Better than that — I'm going to have a baby!'

For a moment Roz just stood looking at her, unable to speak. Then she ran to her mother and threw her arms round her, 'I can't believe it — it's marvellous. Larry'll be over the moon, it's just what he needs . . . it's just too wonderful . . . ' She was laughing and crying at the same time as she clung to Kate.

'It is for me and I only hope he feels the same, but he's been so moody lately Roz, I know one can't blame him, to him it feels as if he's lost everything, but in many ways he still has more than lots of people, we both have. I don't quite know how to tell him.'

'But you must Mum, as soon as he comes in.'

'Tell him what?'

They both swung round, Larry stood in the doorway, his hands stiffly at his sides. 'Tell me I'm a useless lump of flesh and it's time I pulled myself together and found some kind of job? That I'm a kept man living on my wife's money.'

Roz slipped quickly out of the room as Kate ran to him, gently pulling off his coat and making him sit down. She bent and dried Fred's muddy paws on an old towel, pushing a mug of coffee in front of Larry. Awkwardly he fumbled to pick it up, spilling some of the liquid on the scrubbed wood of the kitchen table, putting the mug back again with an oath of impatience.

'Well, come on, what's so important that Roz said I must be told?'

For a moment she didn't answer, then she sat down opposite him drawing little circles with her finger, where he'd spilt the liquid on the table. She tried to talk calmly, but the words rose and burst out of her like bubbles. 'I . . . we're going to have a baby Larry. I saw the doctor this morning, there isn't any doubt.'

He sat staring at the mess on the table, painfully turning his hands over and gazing at the fingers with their livid scars . . . then suddenly he dropped his head on to them with a little moan, 'Oh Kate, why does it have to be now, now that I'm useless, now that I can't even keep a small baby, let alone pay for a child's education . . . all of it will have to come from you.'

Swiftly she got up and went round to

him, 'Don't, my darling. Don't torture yourself like this, it isn't necessary. I thought you'd be so pleased, overjoyed like I am. It's a kind of miracle Larry, Doctor Clarke himself could hardly believe it — it hardly ever happens to a woman when she's had the kind of treatment I did. But it's true, it's our child, don't you understand that? A result of our love, our second honeymoon, you called it, that time in America . . . it's what we've both longed for to complete our happiness.'

'I know,' he groaned, 'that's why it's so awful, so unbearable, if only it happened before my accident, when I was a whole man, I'm no more than half a man now.' He raised his face and looked at her with pain in his eyes, and suddenly she realized how terribly thin his face had grown in the last few weeks. She cradled his head against her breast as if he were a baby himself, murmuring endearments and words of comfort, until at last he smiled at her.

But life wasn't easy. Larry slipped

from mood to mood like cloud shadows on summer grass, while Kate was bursting with happiness and contentment. Life had taken on a new meaning, and she and Roz spent hours on baby talk.

'Won't it be priceless Tom having an uncle younger than himself — or an aunt?' Roz laughed, 'Somehow I keep thinking of the baby as a boy — I can't imagine having a girl in the family.'

Kate smiled, 'You were a baby girl yourself love!'

'I know, and I just can't believe this baby will be my small half sister or brother — or is it step? It'll be super having two young babies,' she looked grave for a moment, 'I'm sure Larry'll feel different when it's actually born.' She paused, for she had said those very words once before about another birth, and that time they hadn't proved to be true.

Now the weeks seemed to fly, and from what Doctor Clarke could tell, the baby would be due about the end of November.

'What a Christmas it'll be! All nappies and bottles,' Roz giggled.

Just lately Larry had been even more preoccupied than usual, and then suddenly one morning he said, 'When I was at the hospital last week I heard of a new man in London, he does wonders with burns and rehabilitation, I think I'll go and see him.' He looked away for a moment, 'At least I ought to be able to hold my own son in my arms.'

Kate smiled, thankful that at last he was taking a bit of interest in the baby. 'That's a marvellous idea, I'll drive you up.'

He drew her into his arms, 'No you won't, love. You're going to stay right here, near the hospital and the doctor who knows all about you, I'm not risking you — and my child.' He bent and kissed her gently on the lips, 'Roz'll drive me to the station, it's an easy journey on the train, and anyway this time of the year the weather can be dodgy for a long trip in the car.'

Kate knew it was a constant annoyance to him that he couldn't drive the car any distance now, he could manage short journeys into town, but the strain on the stiff fingers was intolerable after a time, she'd changed the car for one with an automatic box so there was no difficulty with the gears, but he still couldn't grip the steering wheel.

So it was arranged. The specialist would give Larry a preliminary examination and tell him if he thought there was any chance of his being able to help him, then if so, a course of treatment, or even an operation if it was necessary.

He left in high spirits, somehow he seemed confident now that this new man would be able to help him, he was much more cheerful than he had been for ages as though the thought of the coming child had at last spurred him to make a fresh effort.

The sky was overcast and leaden, there was a bite in the east wind like ice, and Kate was glad when Roz got back from the station.

'I think it's going to snow Mum, I got in some extra food just in case, you know how easily we get cut off in this narrow lane if a blizzard should start.'

For a moment Kate felt a little twinge of fear, of apprehension. Supposing they were cut off and the baby started to come . . . but that was ridiculous, it wasn't due for another three weeks at least. She'd been to the clinic only the day before and the examination had shown that everything was perfectly normal, and she'd never felt better. She mustn't turn into a fusspot in her old age! But it was just an over anxiety that nothing should go wrong for Larry's sake as much as anything.

'What's the matter Mum? You look so serious, are you feeling O.K.?'

She smiled reassuringly, 'Never better.'

Later that night when she took Fred out for his last run, a few fine flakes of snow fell on her upturned face, it fell quietly, relentlessly and the sky was dark and sullen. She was glad Roz had filled the log box on the patio and that they had plenty of food. She only hoped the lane wouldn't get blocked before Larry came back. He'd rung earlier to say he'd arrived safely, the hotel was very comfortable and he had an appointment at ten the next morning with the specialist.

Kate went to bed feeling pleasantly drowsy and content. She could hear the wind rising, beating itself and moaning against the old walls of the mill. It sounded like a wailing banshee and she snuggled down into the pleasant warmth of the sheets.

The snow itself made no sound as it fell swiftly, heavily now, piling against hedges and trees.

She dreamt she was being chased by something evil, terrifying. She could feel its hot breath on her neck, but she couldn't move . . . as if her feet were rooted to the ground. The thing, whatever it was, lifted a gleaming knife and then swiftly plunged it downwards

. . . she tried to scream but no sound would come . . . there was only this agonizing pain, and the feeling of falling, whirling into space, round and round . . . she was wet, soaking wet and cold.

For a few moments when she opened her eyes she couldn't think where she was, then a wonderful relief flooded her as she realized it had been a dream — but she was wet . . . then a pain like an iron hand gripped her in a vice — that hadn't been a dream . . . she let out a little gasp of anguish. It was remembered pain now — a contraction . . . the baby must be starting, their calculations had been wrong, or else it was premature. She dragged herself up the bed. Then she saw the reason why she was damp, the window had slipped its catch and was banging open, the room was full of an unnaturally bright light, an utter quiet hung over everything. She shivered filled with a terrible, unreasonable loneliness . . . she was being ridiculous, Roz was only a few steps away . . . she reached out and switched on the bedside light. The snow had blown in through the window and was melting on the bed and the carpet. The next contraction didn't hurt much, but it took her by surprise and she tried to bite back another gasp of pain . . . and then the waters broke and she said, 'Oh God!' She sat on the edge of the bed feeling for her slippers. She could see the moon shining outside, it must have stopped snowing. She got to her feet, she must get to the phone, wake Roz. It was then she looked out of the window and saw the snow . . . piled high against the trees and hedges in the moonlight. It must be at least three or four feet, even where it hadn't drifted. In the lane it would be deeper.

Still, she reassured herself, in the jet age people didn't get cut off, snow ploughs, bulldozers, helicopters — all the modern life savers could swiftly be put in motion. It would only be a matter of an hour or two — but how much time had she? Desperately she tried to think back to Roz's birth — how long had it been before the baby appeared after the waters broke? It all seemed vague now . . . she'd been comfortably settled in a hospital, they'd given her something to make her sleep, Tom had been with her. Now she longed for Larry. He'd be heart broken if his child arrived without his being there — he'd been determined to stay with her all through the birth.

Another pain doubled her up so that the nails of her hand bit deep into the palm. Somehow she dragged herself out into the passage and along to Roz's door. She opened it softly, 'Roz, it's me darling, could you phone for the doctor, the baby's started.'

Roz shot out of bed like an arrow from the bow. She put her arm round Kate. 'You've no business to be out of bed, it's freezing.'

Kate nodded, 'I know, it's been snowing, pretty heavily by the look of it. Must have been doing it for some time.'

Roz glanced at her watch. 'It's half

past four. I heard the wind, but I never thought . . . well, not to worry. We'll soon have you safely in hospital. Can you manage to get back to bed? I'll slip on my slacks and a sweater and ring for the ambulance, unless you'd rather I drove you in.'

Kate shook her head, 'No, it would mean disturbing Tom, putting him in his carrycot, but I think you'd better hurry love.' She gasped and gripped Roz's arm as another pain bit like a sharp toothed animal. The contractions were getting stronger — and more frequent. She ought to try to pack her case . . . but her limbs seemed to be weighted with lead.

She didn't know how long she lay in bed, waiting for Roz, trying to count the time between the pains . . . she seemed to swing away into unconsciousness at times . . . she thought Larry stood by her, holding her hand, encouraging her to be brave . . . then she opened her eyes and saw Roz. She smiled at her, 'Everything O.K.?'

But Roz's face was white with apprehension.

'Don't worry darling,' Kate tried to sound reassuring. 'I'll hang on till they get here — don't want to make you into a maternity nurse do we?' She tried to grin but guessed the pain must have made a travesty of it. Roz still didn't speak. Kate closed her eyes wearily as another pain shot through her.

Then she heard the words that Roz uttered very softly . . . as if she hoped her very tone would make them untrue . . . she tried to persuade herself they hadn't been said, that she was dreaming again.

'It's no use Mum. The phone's out of order, and I tried to get the car out, but it's no use, I can't even get to the garage, let alone open the doors, the snow's built right up against them, it'll take hours to shift.'

She didn't add she'd nearly fallen into the already swollen and swiftly flowing leat.

Somehow Kate dragged herself into a

sitting position. 'Then we'll just have to manage.' She racked her brains, 'Get plenty of hot water, and bowls, towels, rags anything . . . old sheets and cotton wool, scissors and thread . . . all we can do is keep our fingers crossed and hope there aren't any complications and we can manage between us.' The words were cut off as once more she gave a gasp of pain and swung away into the now familiar pit of black agony.

The next few hours — or they might have been days for all Kate knew — were a jumble of pain, exhaustion, of Roz's horrified face looking down at her — of trying to talk, to tell her what to do — but really she knew so little herself, she'd never actually seen a baby born, and Roz's birth had been 20 years ago. Maybe what the girl did was instinctive, she did what she felt she had to do . . . all Kate remembered was the pain and the burning anxiety that whatever happened, the baby would be all right, for Larry's sake. At last she heard the thin wail, the little smack as

Roz made the baby cry, then she let herself go, be whirled away again, but this time into blessed painless, warm darkness.

When she woke the sun streamed through the window, the ceiling was bright with the reflection of the snow, and a fire burned brightly in the grate. She could hear a thin crying somewhere near, she turned her head and Roz was standing looking down at her. She knelt down by the bed, 'Oh Mum, are you all right? I thought you would die, it was awful.' She buried her head in the sheet while Kate stroked her hair.

'I'm fine love, just a bit tired, how about the baby?'

Roz raised her head and looked at her, joy shining through the tears, 'He's beautiful, a perfect little boy. And he's got masses of dark hair just like Larry . . . I think he's really prettier than Tom was even when he was born,' she added gravely, so that Kate had to smile. Roz lifted the baby from his cot — the cot Kate had lovingly prepared in the weeks she'd been waiting for him to arrive. She took the warm bundle into her arms. As she looked down at the small wrinkled face, so like a crumpled rose petal, she held out her other hand and took Roz's.

'Darling, how can Larry and I ever thank you for what you did? If you hadn't been here, and kept your head, anything might have happened, I'd never have managed on my own!'

Roz smiled, 'Well you may not remember, but in between the times you passed out, you were giving me detailed instructions just like a bossy Sister in hospital! If I hadn't been so busy, and so frightened, I'd have had to laugh!'

Kate lay back against the pillows, smiling at her, her son safely in her arms. She'd examined him carefully, he was perfect as far as one could tell. 'Must have been instinct, for both of us.' She held the baby to her breast, 'Come on young man, we'd better feed you before you wake your nephew!'

It was late afternoon by the time a snow plough got through to them with milk from the neighbouring farm. Roz told the driver what had happened and asked him to fetch the doctor for the phone was still out of order.

Within the hour Doctor Clarke arrived, with an ambulance, but when he saw a smiling Kate with her lusty son lying in the crook of her arm, he was almost speechless.

'Do you want to go into hospital Kate? Or shall I try to get the District Nurse to come and keep an eye on you?'

Kate grinned at Roz, 'I don't think hospital is necessary, I have a very efficient nurse here!'

'Oh Mum, I couldn't bear the two of you to go away now,' Roz said, 'unless you think you should.'

'Well you've done a marvellous job,' Doctor Clarke said, 'and I can see they're in good hands, the snow's starting to thaw already and no more is forecast — I'll get in touch with the telephone people right away.'

Kate thought of Larry — he wouldn't even know he had a son and by this time he would have seen the specialist and perhaps had his verdict . . . if he tried to phone and found he couldn't get through he'd be anxious . . . she gave Doctor Clarke his number.

'I'd like to have told him myself,' she smiled, 'but at least coming from you he'll have to believe I'm O.K. Tell him just to get home as soon as he can . . . his family need him.'

* * *

Next day Larry stood looking down at his son.

'He's just beautiful,' was all he could say, over and over again as he gazed at him, lying in Kate's arms.

Gently he lifted up one tiny fist, uncurling the fingers and examining each one.

'Even his nails are perfect,' he smiled in amazement.

Kate burst out laughing. 'Of course, what did you expect?'

As if he hadn't heard her, he went on, 'Maybe he'll be an artist, use those hands to paint.'

'Darling,' Kate said softly, 'From what you tell me you'll not only be able to teach him, but you yourself will be painting again before long.'

He smiled, 'Who knows? They only hope — they don't really know, but it won't matter now, here's my reason for living, you and my son . . . that's love, true love, and neither age nor distance nor time can take that away.'

Kate smiled up at him, 'Do you remember I once quoted Edward Dowson to you — 'They are not long — the weeping and the laughter'. Somehow they seem to have taken on a new meaning — I always thought it just meant that *all* our days here were short — but perhaps what he really meant was that each day, each hour even, can vary so much that it brings laughter and tears in turn and that neither last for long.'

He bent and kissed her, 'How well that describes our life together.'

And Roz coming softly to the door saw the two dark heads of father and son each side of Kate and thought, at last all the family were indeed come home.

THE END

Other titles in the
Linford Romance Library:

VISIONS OF THE HEART

Christine Briscomb

When property developer Connor Grant contracted Natalie Jensen to landscape the grounds of his large country house near Ashley in South Australia, she was ecstatic. But then she discovered he was acquiring — and ripping apart — great swathes of the town. Her own mother's house and the hall where the drama group met were two of his targets. Natalie was desperate to stop Connor's plans — but she also had to fight the powerful attraction flowing between them.